"So who is he, then, your secret fiancé?"

Kalera knocked over the pen holder she was needlessly repositioning. "He's successful, has his own company.... He's also kind, generous and good to his mother."

Duncan looked skeptical. "Not cut the apron strings yet? Is he much younger than you?"

"As a matter of fact, he's exactly *your* age."

"Is this your coy way of telling me you're panting with unrequited love for me?"

Kalera's gray eyes flashed silver. "My God, you are so *arrogant!*"

Duncan shrugged. "Comes with the territory," he murmured. "You know— mid-thirties, good-looking, clever, stinking rich...." His voice dropped to a sexy purr. "Not to mention sizzling in bed. Tell me, Kalera, what has your mystery man got that I haven't?"

SUSAN NAPIER was born on St. Valentine's Day, so it's not surprising she has developed an enduring love of romantic stories. She started her writing career as a journalist in Auckland, New Zealand, trying her hand at romance fiction only after she had married her handsome boss! Numerous books later, she still lives with her most enduring hero, two future heroes—her sons!—two cats and a computer. When she's not writing, she likes to read and cook, often simultaneously!

Susan Napier writes deliciously sensual romances, with heroes to die for and a romantic intensity that will leave you breathless!

Books by Susan Napier

HARLEQUIN PRESENTS®
1788—THE SISTER SWAP
1847—RECKLESS CONDUCT
1870—A LESSON IN SEDUCTION
1918—MISTRESS OF THE GROOM
1985—HONEYMOON BABY

Don't miss any of our special offers. Write to us at the following address for information on our newest releases.

Harlequin Reader Service
U.S.: 3010 Walden Ave., P.O. Box 1325, Buffalo, NY 14269
Canadian: P.O. Box 609, Fort Erie, Ont. L2A 5X3

SUSAN NAPIER

In Bed with the Boss

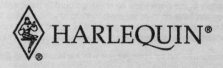

TORONTO • NEW YORK • LONDON
AMSTERDAM • PARIS • SYDNEY • HAMBURG
STOCKHOLM • ATHENS • TOKYO • MILAN • MADRID
PRAGUE • WARSAW • BUDAPEST • AUCKLAND

If you purchased this book without a cover you should be aware that this book is stolen property. It was reported as "unsold and destroyed" to the publisher, and neither the author nor the publisher has received any payment for this "stripped book."

ISBN 0-373-12009-5

IN BED WITH THE BOSS

First North American Publication 1999.

Copyright © 1998 by Susan Napier.

All rights reserved. Except for use in any review, the reproduction or utilization of this work in whole or in part in any form by any electronic, mechanical or other means, now known or hereafter invented, including xerography, photocopying and recording, or in any information storage or retrieval system, is forbidden without the written permission of the publisher, Harlequin Enterprises Limited, 225 Duncan Mill Road, Don Mills, Ontario, Canada M3B 3K9.

All characters in this book have no existence outside the imagination of the author and have no relation whatsoever to anyone bearing the same name or names. They are not even distantly inspired by any individual known or unknown to the author, and all incidents are pure invention.

This edition published by arrangement with Harlequin Books S.A.

® and TM are trademarks of the publisher. Trademarks indicated with ® are registered in the United States Patent and Trademark Office, the Canadian Trade Marks Office and in other countries.

Printed in U.S.A.

CHAPTER ONE

'WHAT in the hell is this?'

In spite of the fact that she had been conducting a mental countdown, Kalera Martin still jumped as the door to the adjoining office crashed back against the wall, sending a concussive shock vibrating around the room.

She sat straight in her swivel chair, her hands involuntarily pressing down on the stack of folders which she was in the process of sorting into neat piles on her orderly desk.

The man standing in the doorway waving a sheet of paper in his clenched fist looked anything but orderly. The expensive, custom-made clothes could not subdue the sheer physicality of his adrenaline-charged personality. Even in an uncharacteristically conservative pinpoint oxford shirt, navy trousers, dark blue silk tie and navy braces, Duncan Royal managed to look more like a menacing street thug than the owner of a multi-million-dollar high-tech company. He was intimidatingly tall and broad and, when the brilliance of his argument failed to get him his own way, was not above shamelessly using his impressive size as an added negotiating tool, browbeating stubborn opponents into changing their minds in order to stay on his good side.

Right now his good side was nowhere in evidence. The killer good looks were marred by a fierce scowl, the jet-black hair which was usually raked sleekly back behind his ears tumbled across his thunderous brow, outrage pouring off him in aggressive waves as he glared across the room at the slender, dainty woman behind the desk.

On the off chance that he hadn't yet reached the bottom of his morning mail Kalera raised her finely arched eyebrows in cautious enquiry.

'I don't know—what is it?' she asked in the deep, husky voice that always surprised people, coming as it did from such a small frame.

'You tell me!' he snarled, storming over to throw the offending paper down in front of her with a furious flick of his powerful wrist.

Kalera caught the page before it wafted to the floor and smoothed it out with fingers that she was relieved to note didn't tremble at all.

'Well?' He loomed over her accusingly.

She cleared her throat and looked up, her cool grey eyes clashing with his incendiary gaze.

'It's my letter of resignation—'

He made a harsh, growling sound in the back of his throat. 'I know what it *is*—'

'Well, then, why did you ask?' she dared to ask mildly. 'I would have thought it was self-explanatory.'

She held the letter out to him but he ignored it, bending abruptly to plant his lean, manicured hands flat on the edge of her desk, thrusting his face towards her, giving her a close-up view of the shock, rage and disbelief seething in the midnight-blue eyes.

'Then you thought wrong!'

Kalera watched, fascinated, as the small nerve which fluttered at the corner of his narrow mouth was compressed by the clenching of muscles along his rigid jaw. She felt pummelled by the force of his concentrated psychic energy.

This was a first.

In the three years that she had worked at Labyrinth Technology as his secretary Kalera had frequently witnessed Duncan Royal explode, but she had never been the direct target of one of his infamous fiery tantrums.

Perhaps it was because her delicate build made him overtly aware of his own vastly superior size and strength, or perhaps it was the dampening effect of her cool serenity in the face of emotional scenes, but on the rare occasions that Kalera had slipped up and given him just cause to display his volatile temperament he had chosen to vent his spleen on the inanimate objects around him rather than on her remorseful blonde head.

To her certain knowledge this transference of his hostility had so far cost the company a pot plant, a cellphone, two coffee cups, a pen-holder and a terse lecture from a fire safety officer after Duncan had dramatically set fire to one of Kalera's memos, causing a minor conflagration in his waste-paper basket which set off the smoke alarms and led to the evacuation of the entire building.

'Well?'

He lunged closer, his eyes snapping with impatience, and Kalera leaned back in her chair in a vain attempt to distance herself from his angry aura. 'Uh…which part don't you understand?' she murmured, wincing inwardly at the lame response. It bore no resemblance to the crisp, assertive statements which she had rehearsed in front of her mirror that morning. She hated scenes and had been hoping that her carefully worded letter would soothe rather than inflame, diplomatically preparing the way for her more daunting confession.

Alas, her temperamental boss thrived on confrontations. Full and forceful frankness was his preferred operating style and a civilised conversation was clearly not on this morning's agenda.

'Every damned part! The whole thing is incomprehensible!' Duncan Royal was used to understanding instantly complex equations, concepts and problems, both real and abstract. The brilliance of his intellect usually put him in control of his environment. He didn't like being reduced to common human bewilderment.

Kalera screwed up her courage. 'Well, I—'

'Two paragraphs!' he interrupted, his deep, rasping voice fierce with indignation as his big shoulders shifted and he stabbed at the offending letter with a vicious forefinger. 'Damn you, Kalera, after all this time is that all you consider I deserve? *Two measly paragraphs* to tell me that one of my most trusted employees is walking out on me!'

Kalera nervously tucked a stray strand of sun-streaked blonde hair back into the smooth sweep of the elegant French roll she wore to work. Her narrow oval face, which Harry had been fond of telling her reminded him of that of a Madonna in a medieval painting—smooth, serene, mysterious—revealed nothing of her clammy apprehension.

She knew how much personal loyalty meant to Duncan Royal; it was the rock on which he had founded his enormous success. The computer industry was a cutthroat business in which paranoia ran rife. Duncan had made a fortune out of developing software products that caught larger competitors napping and an essential part of his strategy was to personally hand-pick his employees—right down to the office cleaners! Nothing was contracted out, except to other branches of his business. As a result he had gathered around him a group of extremely dedicated and ambitious men and women who were richly rewarded for their total commitment to their brilliant but eccentric leader.

Prepared as she had been for an objection to her decision to resign, Kalera was taken aback by the violence of Duncan's reaction. She knew that she was good at her job because he was as quick to praise as he was to anger, but she was hardly irreplaceable. It wasn't as if she was one of his resident computer geniuses, or in any way unique in her organisational skills; she was simply a useful cog in his administrative machine.

Surely he couldn't already *know*...?

'You make it sound as if I'm quitting without notice,' she protested. 'But I'm not leaving you in the lurch—I did say I'm quite happy to work out the four weeks stated in my contract—'

'Damn your contract; you know that's not what I'm talking about!' he thundered.

She stiffened. Just because she disliked scenes, that didn't mean she was afraid to stand up for herself. 'There's no need to shout, Duncan,' she said coldly. 'I'm not deaf—'

'No, just dumb!' He slammed a frustrated fist on the desk with a force that rattled her computer keyboard.

'If I'm that stupid then you should be pleased to see me go,' she snapped, guiltily aware that her offer to work her notice was merely a token gesture. Once he found out the truth, Duncan wouldn't want her within a mile of his hallowed domain.

'Not *that* sort of dumb!' He started to pace. 'You couldn't talk this over with me first? What...am I so inaccessible...so impossible to talk to that you couldn't even bring yourself to mention that you were thinking of leaving?'

He stopped in front of her desk again, his arms shooting out wide as his incredulous tone denounced the sheer ridiculousness of the notion. He had an open-door policy towards his staff and most of them took full advantage of the opportunity to express their opinions and ideas freely.

Kalera's thick lashes swept down to conceal the expression in her soft grey eyes as she concentrated on folding and re-folding the edge of the letter. 'I'm sorry...but, after all, it was my decision to make. It had nothing to do with you—'

She realised as soon as the words were out of her mouth that she had made a tactical error.

'Are you trying to tell me that it's none of my business when an employee quits out of the blue, without even bothering to give a reason?' Duncan exploded afresh. 'No, dammit, *not* just an employee—a *friend*, Kalera...'

A wave of fresh guilt swept over her as a dark-complexioned face framed by a profusion of short Rasta braids and beads suddenly popped around the open door that was the main entrance to Kalera's office.

'Hey, girl, what's all this racket—? Oh, hi, Chief, I should have known it would be you... From the sound of it, I thought Kalera had a pack of Rottweilers loose in here!'

Duncan glared at his young assistant's irreverent grin. 'Do you mind, Anna? You're interrupting a private conversation.'

'Oh, really?' Anna Ihaka advanced into the doorway, her coffee-coloured eyes darting eagerly from one to the other. 'What about?'

'I'll tell you later,' said Kalera hurriedly, hearing Duncan's breath rattle ominously in his throat.

'Oh, OK—give me a buzz when he's finished his rant and I'll bring you a cup of coffee.' Anna was incurably cheerful and totally unsquashable, the perfect assistant for a man who, in a bad mood, was the Sultan of Squash.

'I'll just close this door for you on my way out, then, shall I, Chief?' she added sweetly. 'Only, we can hear the punctuation marks in your *private conversation* all over the floor, you see, and it's a bit off-putting for poor Bryan who's trying to give a demo and impress some very snooty clients with our discretion.' She snicked the door smartly shut before he could get in the last word.

'I'm going to wring that girl's neck one of these days,' growled Duncan, and saw the expression on Kalera's face. 'What have you got to smirk about?'

Kalera hastily straightened the wayward corners of her mouth. She had obviously handled this all wrong, but perhaps it wasn't too late to amend her error. 'Look, there's a very good reason for my wanting to leave—' she began huskily.

'Really? Did I miss something?' He leaned over and plucked the letter out of her fidgeting fingers, unravelling the folds and reading from it with a deadly sarcasm which mocked the stark formality of the words:

'"I have enjoyed my term of employment with Labyrinth Technology—" *Huh!*' His snort was eloquent with contempt for her flattering opening. '"But due to a change in my personal circumstances I regret to inform you that I wish to tender my resignation with such notice as required under the terms of my contract." Change in personal circumstances?' he lowered the page to repeat furiously. 'What in the hell is *that* supposed to mean?'

Kalera moistened her suddenly dry lips with a little flick of her tongue. Was it better to blurt it out, or lead up to it gently? She was no longer certain.

While she hesitated, Duncan was already darting ahead with his customary impatience.

'You can't have got a better job,' he decided with arrogant confidence. 'This one is tailor-made for your talents—after all, you virtually designed it yourself when you came to work for me. You're much more than just a secretary; you manage the whole office. You've always seemed to enjoy working with me. Is it the money? Have you decided I don't pay you enough?'

The question was absurd. Duncan might be possessive about his ideas, but he was notoriously over-generous with money. He drove his accountants mad with his insistence on sharing his profits with his employees via bonuses, gifts and royalty percentages on software which they had helped to develop. So well did he treat his workers that no competitor had yet succeeded in bribing or head-hunting away a Labyrinth employee.

'Yes, of course you do. But I—'

'Aren't you happy here?'

If he stopped peppering her with questions she might be able to get out a satisfactory answer. 'I've been very happy here, but—'

'But! But what?' he cut in roughly. 'But you're not now? Why? Is there some problem you haven't been telling me about? Your working conditions and environment haven't changed, so what else could it be?' His lightning-fast brain sorted through the possible options and his eyes suddenly narrowed threateningly. 'Has someone been harassing you?'

She was bewildered by his sudden change in tack. 'Harassing me?'

'Sexually. Making suggestive remarks, brushing up against you, touching you, that kind of thing—making you feel unsafe at work?'

Her mouth opened and closed and she flushed with mortification.

He pounced. 'My God, that's it, isn't it?' He rounded the desk and swivelled her chair to face him, ignoring her squeak of surprise as he crouched in front of her and picked her limp left hand out of her lap.

'Who is it?' He sandwiched her hand between his smooth, warm palms and lowered his voice coaxingly. 'Did he threaten you in some way? Tell me, Kalera, and no matter who it turns out to be I'll sort the bastard out. I'll fire him so fast his feet won't touch the ground!'

His dark blue eyes roved down over her figure, inspecting the soft draping of her lemon silk blouse and narrow green linen skirt as if he somehow expected to see the culprit's fingerprints emblazoned on the fabric. There was something almost possessive about the protective survey and a wave of unwelcome warmth swept over Kalera's skin as his frowning gaze skimmed over the firm thrust of her small breasts. She sternly smothered a little thrill of illicit awareness with the ease of long practice and took a huffing breath.

'For goodness' sake, Duncan, will you shut up and let me explain? I'm not being harassed!' She tried to tug her hand from his but he wouldn't let her go.

'Then why are you blushing?'

'Because I'm embarrassed that you could think I wouldn't know how to handle a simple case of sexual harassment by myself.'

He scowled, his thumb absently rubbing over her captured fingers. 'You shouldn't have to handle it on your own; that's the point.'

'Well, it's a moot point because, as I said, no one's harassing me—' She stopped, disconcerted, as his expression froze into shocked stillness.

Did he think she was lying? Goodness, surely he didn't really believe that Kalera was so irresistibly alluring that she must inevitably be the target of sexual predators! Although she was passably attractive she wasn't the type of woman to drive men to extremes. When she refused to respond to their overtures they typically backed off with a shrug. And at work, taking the lead from their boss, the males had always treated her with a friendliness tempered by respect.

She frowned as she reached the only logical reason for him to jump to such a ridiculous conclusion. 'Why are you asking me this—have you received a complaint about someone in the office?'

Duncan wasn't listening. His head had snapped down and he was staring at the bare fingers of her left hand.

'You've taken off your wedding and engagement rings!' His voice was hoarse with disbelief as his thumb probed the smooth, slightly shiny white band of flesh which contrasted with the light tan of the rest of her hand. His normally mobile and expressive features retained their frozen blankness as he demanded, 'Why aren't you wearing Harry's rings?'

Kalera's newly exposed skin was proving to be uncomfortably sensitive and the light rasping of the pad of Duncan's thumb against the tiny indentations in her finger sent a feathery tingle shooting up her arm.

'They're in my drawer at home... I thought—it was time to put them away,' she stumbled, her fingers curling into her palm, forming a small fist that silently rejected the disturbing nature of his touch.

He withdrew it instantly, but instead of rising to his feet he rocked slightly back on the balls of his feet, his bent knees brushing the sides of her calves as he steadied himself by placing his hands on the arms of her chair. His rigid expression thawed, a dark emotion flaring in the navy eyes as he looked up into her flushed face.

'Past time,' he agreed, and the hint of satisfaction in his tone made her stiffen defensively, twisting her hands in her lap.

'I'll never forget Harry—'

'Of course you won't. But he died two years ago...you didn't,' he said with his usual devastating bluntness. 'You have nothing to feel uneasy about, Kalera. You honoured his memory with a decent period of mourning...' His voice softened. 'You honoured both of them. Now you're obviously ready to move on—to start looking at all the opportunities life has to offer a woman of today.'

His mouth curved into an approving smile. It was the perfect opening and she eagerly snatched it.

'I'm glad you think so, because that's exactly what's happened,' she said, taking a deep breath before she announced, 'I got engaged last night.'

'You what?' He was still smiling—that faint, whimsical, sexy crook of his lips that had women toppling for him like ninepins—and Kalera could see him thinking that he had obviously misheard.

'Last night...someone I've been seeing...I—he asked me to marry him...'

She faltered to a stop as she was witness to a sight unique in her experience: Duncan Royal stunned speechless. He looked like a man who had been hit over the head with a mallet. His quizzical smile vanished and his jaw sagged. His mouth opened and closed but the only sound that came out was a breathy wheeze. His olive complexion paled, accentuating the twin crescents of darker skin curving below the inner corners of his eyes and making him look as haggard as he was handsome. If it hadn't been for his anchoring grip on her chair Kalera got the distinct impression that he would have toppled on his backside on the carpet.

He was, quite literally, floored!

In any other circumstances Kalera would have been highly amused. Duncan enjoyed jolting people out of their complacency and dropping verbal bombshells was one of his favourite methods of hijacking conversations. To turn the tables on him so effectively was quite a considerable feat. But she knew the peaceful state of suspended animation would not last very long.

'We went out to dinner and he asked me to marry him and I said yes,' she expanded hastily, hoping to stave off the barrage of questions she could see forming in his eyes. 'So when I got home I took my old rings off. I can't very well wear them when I'm engaged to someone else...although maybe I'll wear the solitaire as a dress ring later, when—after we're married...'

Duncan's unblinking gaze moved down to her slender right hand, curled protectively at her waist, and she realised that he was seeking concrete proof of her claim.

'I haven't got a new engagement ring yet because we're going to choose it together—tonight after work, as a matter of fact...'

Duncan shook his head once, violently, like a seasoned fighter emerging from a standing count. For once his intellect was lagging far behind the pace as he said slowly, 'You've been seeing someone else?'

Kalera's shoulders twitched in an awkward shrug. 'As you just pointed out, Harry's been gone two years now—'

'You've been seeing another *man*?'

And to think Kalera had always felt inferior to his towering intellect! She couldn't stop a bubble of nervous laughter escaping her throat. 'Well, I certainly haven't been dating other *women*. Besides, same-sex marriages are illegal, so there wouldn't be much point in my becoming engaged to—'

Her feeble joke didn't even bring a glimmer of humour to his expression. If anything it seemed to stoke his outrage.

'You've been *dating*?' He shoved her chair so it skidded back on its casters and stood up, fists planted on his lean hips. 'Just how long has this been going on?'

'A few months,' she confessed, although in practical terms it had actually been much less than that.

His dark brows snapped together. 'A few months! You've been seeing other men for *months* without even mentioning it?'

He made it sound as if she had been living a secret life of rampant promiscuity. One minute he was urging her to get over losing Harry, the next he was making her feel guilty for pre-empting his advice.

'Not *men*,' she protested, flushed with a mixture of guilt and indignance. 'A *man*. Singular. And, well, it all started so casually there wasn't really anything *to* mention…and, anyway, why should I? You don't talk to *me* about the women that *you* date!'

'That's because—' He broke off, and his eyes narrowed on her pink face. 'No, I don't, but that doesn't prevent you knowing about them, does it? You field my calls, open my mail and have access to my diary and hard drive, and what you don't know I'm sure the grapevine provides—this place is a hotbed of internal gossip and the network bulletin board seems to keep well up to date with jokes about my social life. I bet you end up knowing the women in my life better than I do!'

'I doubt it,' murmured Kalera sardonically, thinking of the progression of Body Beautifuls who had been photographed hanging on his arm, although, given Duncan's legendary restlessness and the average tenure of his girlfriends, the idea wasn't entirely far-fetched.

'Oh, I didn't mean in the carnal sense,' he said, his gravelly voice outrageousness in its blandness as he segued smoothly into his interrogation. 'So, who is he, then? This wonderful man who so *casually* infiltrated your life that he wasn't worth mentioning to your friends?' His expression hardened. 'Or am I just the last to find out?'

Kalera shook her head. Unable to bear the inactivity, she pretended to straighten things on her desk. 'No, I haven't talked about him to anyone. It's—rather awkward...'

He perched his hip on the edge of her desk, propping an elbow on the top of her VDU, the dark, pin-striped fabric of his trousers pulling taut across his long, muscular thigh as he absently hitched his polished heel onto the handle of her file drawer.

'Why? Is he already married?'

She almost choked on her appalled gasp. 'No!'

'Divorced? Children kicking up a stink about Dad's new girlfriend? No? Maybe you're ashamed of him,' he speculated, seeming to relish the idea. 'Is he some kind of sleazy low-life you're embarrassed to be seen with in public?'

Kalera knocked over the pen-holder she was needlessly repositioning. 'No! Of course not,' she denied, concentrating fiercely on rearranging the pens. 'He's very well-educated and successful. He has his own company...'

She waited for him to ask what line of business her

new fiancé was in, but Duncan proved infuriatingly uncooperative.

'So...he's rich, then?' he drawled, with the hint of a
sneer.

He was purposely being provoking and Kalera was
determined not to be provoked. 'Yes.'

'Good-looking?'

'Very.'

'Intelligent?'

'Extremely.'

'Good in bed?'

She didn't miss a beat. 'Scintillating.'

He opened his mouth and her patience deserted her as
she added tartly, 'He's also kind, generous, fond of
young children and animals and good to his mother.'

He pursed his lips and looked patronisingly sceptical.
'Not cut the apron-strings yet? Is he much younger than
you?'

'Since I'm only twenty-seven, how much younger
could he be?' she snapped, bristling at the idea that she
was the victim of a feminine mid-life crisis. 'He's not
some smooth-talking gigolo or toy-boy if that's what
you're implying. He happens to be in the prime of his
life!'

'What an interesting euphemism,' he needled slyly,
enjoying her small flare of temper. 'I guess that means
he's more the sugar-daddy type.'

She sucked in her breath. 'As a matter of fact, he's
exactly *your* age.'

His eyelids flickered. 'He sounds exactly like me in
every respect so far. Is this your coyly euphemistic way
of telling me you're panting with unrequited love for
me?'

Her grey eyes flashed silver and she forgot she was
supposed to be placating him. 'You're the last man on
earth I'd want to fall in love with,' she cried, her hands
bunching into fists on top of her desk as she struggled

with an uncharacteristic desire to break things. 'My God, you are so *arrogant*!'

He shrugged, acknowledging the accusation with an insufferable grin of bone-deep confidence. The annoying thing was that his arrogance was largely justified; he seemed destined to excel at whatever he did. He joked about being a computer nerd but he was a far cry from the introverted, pasty-faced, pigeon-chested, techno-freak of popular misconception. At thirty-four Duncan kept himself at a peak of physical fitness in the company gym, and played cut-throat games of squash at a city club, smashing stronger opposition with his erratic brilliance and aggressive will to win.

'Comes with the territory,' he murmured. 'You know—mid-thirties, good-looking, clever, stinking rich, kind to children and animals...' His voice dropped an octave to a sexy purr that ruffled the nerves all the way up and down her spine. 'Not to mention sizzling in bed. Tell me, Kalera, what has your mystery man got that *I* haven't?'

She had said scintillating, not sizzling, but he had substituted the word deliberately. Sizzling had an altogether different connotation. Oh, yes, she could well believe that Duncan Royal could burn up the sheets when he was in the mood.

'Humility!' Kalera's face glowed with a very un-Madonna-like spite as he winced.

'Ouch!' He tried to look humble and failed miserably. 'Whoever he is he sounds far too good to be true.'

'Well, he isn't.'

The ring of sincerity in her voice made the teasing malice die out of his expression and he regarded her over the top of her computer, his dark brows lowered, overshadowing his brooding eyes, his square jaw tense.

'He does exist, then? He's not just a figment of your wishful imagination?'

'Of course he exists!' she said firmly. 'I wouldn't be resigning from my job if he didn't!'

His chin clipped up as if she had hit him. 'Wait a minute; is that the only reason you're resigning—because you're getting married?'

'Staying on isn't really an option…' she began carefully.

He slid off the desk. 'What?' He was genuinely outraged. 'You're giving up a job you love because this paragon of yours doesn't want his wife to work? What is this—the Dark Ages? Why didn't you tell the Neanderthal where to get off?'

'Because it's not like that—'

'What is it like, then? Are you planning to move away, is that it? Doesn't he live in Auckland?'

'Yes, he does, but—'

His brain was already fast-forwarding to other possibilities. He was piecing together her unease, her embarrassment and unaccustomed reluctance to get to the point. He blanched. 'Are you pregnant?'

His eyes bored into her flat stomach with an intensity that suggested he had X-ray vision. Kalera felt a tightening in her womb as she was swamped by a sense of intimate invasion. Instinctively she flattened a protective hand over her abdomen and something dark and dangerous smouldered to life in the piercing navy eyes.

'Did you and your lover get careless? Is that the reason for this indecent rush to the altar? You know, illegitimacy doesn't carry the stigma it used to—'

That was going too far, even for Duncan. Kalera leapt to her feet, her slight body vibrating like a tuning fork as she matched his outrage. 'For goodness' sake, what *rush*? We haven't even discussed a wedding date yet!' she yelled. 'We've only just got engaged. Of *course* I'm not pregnant. Do you know how insulting you are? Believe it or not Stephen *wants* to marry me; he's not doing it out of duty or necessity or because he's been trapped into retrieving my soiled honour. If you'd stop trying to cram words into my mouth you might have time to listen to what I have to say!'

He fell back a pace, colour streaking back into his startled expression. Just as Duncan was famous for his temper, Kalera was renowned for her serene composure. She rarely raised her voice but when she did she used her diaphragm properly, as she had been taught during singing lessons as a child, and her normally warm, husky tones could project a shout of booming authority.

Still, it wasn't in Duncan's nature to be confounded for long. 'So...at last the mystery man has a name,' he shot back. 'What's the rest of it? Is he anyone I'd know?'

Kalera put her hands behind her back, squaring her shoulders proudly. 'Actually, yes. And knowing who it is you'll understand why I have to resign. The man I'm marrying is Stephen Prior,' she announced.

And ducked as Duncan Royal went ballistic.

CHAPTER TWO

'So...how did he take it?'

'Not very well,' said Kalera wryly, watching as her fiancé neatly cracked another crayfish leg between his strong fingers and extracted the meat with minimal fuss. She envied the combination of easy self-confidence and natural fastidiousness that allowed him to make it look so simple.

If Kalera had ordered the crayfish in butter sauce she would have been in grease up to her elbows by now, with all sorts of debris clinging to her face. She loved seafood but had never quite got the hang of tangling politely with crustaceans at the dinner table and in the interests of romance, not to mention her white silk dress and unbound hair, had decided to forgo the restaurant's specialty in favour of discreetly de-boned duckling.

Stephen dabbled his fingers in the lemon-scented bowl of water beside his plate and dried them on his starched white napkin. His gold signet-ring gleamed dully in the candlelight, the only embellishment to his elegant, understated style. His dark, custom-tailored jacket and white shirt were as plain as they were expensive and provided the perfect setting for his lean frame and boyish good looks.

'I take it that's one of your masterly understatements,' he said, picking up his champagne glass and toasting her silently before sipping the contents. Not for the first time Kalera basked in his wonderful manners. Whenever she was with Stephen she was made to feel like a lady, as well as a woman. Harry had been a lovely man and a

22

good husband, but he had been a bit short on social graces. Romantic gestures were simply not his style.

She looked around the plush restaurant, enjoying the novelty of dining in sumptuous surroundings with an escort who provoked envious glances from other women. So far all their meetings and dates had, from necessity, been conducted in discreet, out-of-the-way places where neither of them rated a second glance but now they had finally gone public and Stephen said that he wanted to show her off in style. Now there was no longer a need for secrecy he intended to introduce her to the social whirl. He was proud of his future bride and wanted the world and all his friends to approve his good fortune.

He was already planning for them to host a lavish engagement party and Kalera hoped that she wouldn't disgrace him with her inexperience. She and Harry had lived a very quiet life. Going out to the movies or a neighbourhood café or having a few couples around for a casual barbecue had been typical highlights of their social week whereas Stephen was used to a very different scene. She knew that his divorced first wife had a Fine Arts degree and a social pedigree a mile long, and had been renowned for her parties, and, although he had assured Kalera that he would never make comparisons, others in his circle were bound to judge her by Terri's standards.

'I suppose any man would become upset at the news that his secretary has become engaged to his bitterest rival,' Stephen continued, the intent look in his brown eyes belying the casualness of his tone. 'So how *did* he react?'

Thinking that he had been more than tolerant of her disinclination to talk about her traumatic day, Kalera sighed and put down her fork. At least she had managed to get through most of her meal before Stephen's curiosity burst the bonds of his restraint.

'You want chapter and verse?'

'The highlights will do if anything more is going to compromise your honour,' Stephen said with a rueful smile.

He was clearly dying to know every detail of the encounter, but was equally intent on sticking to the pact that they had made when they first met—no discussions about their work. Stephen's ownership of InfoTech Systems put him in direct competition with Labyrinth and he had been labelled Private Enemy No.1 by Duncan Royal. Although Labyrinth currently held the edge, the fierce battle for a bigger slice of the booming New Zealand market in computerised office systems continued to rage between the two companies, fuelled by the owners' personal animosity.

Initially wary of becoming involved with any man, let alone one who presented a potential conflict of interest, and seriously doubting that Stephen's suggestion of mutual self-censorship would work, Kalera's fears had soon been allayed. He was scrupulous about observing the unwritten rules of their relationship and they found plenty to talk about that didn't involve projects or personnel at Labyrinth and InfoTech.

'It was awful, wasn't it?' he groaned as Kalera hesitated, searching for a tactful way to describe the scene. 'I know I should have insisted on being there when you told him—'

She shuddered at the thought. 'That would only have made things worse. Anyway, you're so much *persona non grata* at Labryinth that you wouldn't have got through the front door. The security guards have your photo.'

'Really? I didn't know that.'

Kalera bit her lip at the slip and he quirked an understanding eyebrow. 'Don't worry, the same kind of precautionary measures apply at InfoTech, except we have Royal's face pasted to our games-room dartboard. You can tell him if you like.'

She could just imagine how *that* tidbit of information would be received. It would merely prove to Duncan that she had lied when she said that she and Stephen never discussed any aspect of their work, let alone anything that would compromise professional ethics on either side. She felt a small spurt of annoyance at the amusement on her fiancé's face. There was nothing funny about departing a job she loved with a cloud over her honour.

'No, thanks, I'm in enough trouble as it is.'

He caught the edge in her voice and smoothly adjusted his expression to one of remorseful concern. 'I'm sorry, darling; I know how difficult this has been for you.' He frowned. 'Are you saying he threatened you?'

He sounded so incredulous that Kalera's bruised sense of humour was warmed back to life by his effort to soothe her wounded sensibilities.

'We *are* talking about Duncan Royal,' she pointed out with a dry chuckle. 'Of *course* he threatened me.'

Stephen didn't share the joke. 'I mean physically. I know how terrifying he can be in one of his rages. When we were at school he used to have the most frightful fits—that was one reason he was never made a prefect in spite of his brilliant academic record—he was simply considered too unstable. And then at university—well, he had a reputation for creating mayhem wherever he went…'

'I knew you were briefly in partnership with him a few years ago, but I didn't realise that your acquaintanceship went right back to your childhood,' said Kalera slowly, aware of a slight sense of unease as it suddenly occurred to her that in spite of the illusion of intimacy created by their secret courtship she still had an awful lot to learn about the man she had promised to marry—and vice versa.

'We both had parents who were fixated on their sons attending the "right school" and since our fathers were Old Boys who had boarded together it was fairly inevitable that we ended up in the same college.' Stephen shrugged dismissively. 'He was an arrogant bastard right from the third form—probably would have been expelled several times over if his father hadn't been a leading QC and a heavy donator to school funds. As a senior his temper even terrorised the teachers.'

'I suppose I must have become desensitised to him over the years,' Kalera murmured, thinking that her own family background had been the perfect training ground for coping with Duncan Royal's lightning-bursts of emotion. 'Even when he's yelling blue murder and throwing furniture—like he was this morning—I've never actually been *scared* of him....'

Stephen leaned forward, his wheat-blond hair burnishing his frowning forehead. 'What exactly was he yelling at you?'

Kalera's mouth turned down at the corners. 'You mean before or after he fired me?'

He looked suitably grave, but unsurprised. 'I'm sorry, darling—I did warn you that was probably what would happen. But at least you don't have to worry about being out of work. Even if he gets nasty and refuses you a reference, you know you can walk into a job at InfoTech tomorrow if you like—all you have to do is say the word...'

However fondly couched, 'I told you so' was still the most aggravating phrase in the English language, decided Kalera, her irritation tempered by the knowledge that Stephen wouldn't be feeling quite so smug by the time she finished her story.

'I did try to lead up to it delicately, but as soon as I mentioned your name he fired me on the spot,' she admitted. 'Then he called up Security and got two beefy guards to escort me out of the building. He wouldn't even let me go back to my desk to get my things—'

Her mortification at her treatment was evident in her face as she remembered how it had felt to be marched off the premises like a common criminal.

Stephen's eyes blazed with sympathy. 'The bastard! But you'd already formally handed in your written resignation, right? You're not going to let him get away with putting it around that you were fired—'

'He won't,' she said, flattered by the unexpected heat of his anger. Sometimes she had worried that Stephen was a little *too* cool and self-restrained, even though it was those qualities about him which she had initially found so appealing. 'Because he changed his mind before I even got out of the building. He rescinded the firing and demanded I work my notice after all.'

'He *what*?' Stephen collapsed back in his seat, looking thunderstruck.

Kalera didn't blame him. The swift volte-face had been totally out of character. One of the strengths of Duncan's charismatic leadership was his ability to make instant decisions based on pure gut instinct, and so rarely did his instincts fail him that he had established a reputation for never failing to act on a snap decision.

'The guards had taken me as far as the front door and were about to fling me out into the snow when Duncan came racing across the foyer and ripped me out of their hands. He told them he'd made a mistake and then he dragged me back up to his office and locked me in.'

'*He did what?*' Stephen's smooth baritone rose sharply and Kalera regretted her flippancy when she noticed the covert glances they were receiving from the surrounding tables.

Stephen noticed too and abruptly lowered his voice. 'My God, he actually locked you in the office with him?'

He looked appalled but there was a tiny thread of speculation in his voice that for no reason at all made

Kalera's whole body flush with heat. She felt the colour
rise in her face and suddenly wished her hair weren't so
long and straight that it flowed like water down the middle of her back instead of drifting in handy thickets
around her face. Her wispy blonde fringe provided little
concealment for her pink cheeks.

'Not him. Just me,' she hastened to explain. 'He
pushed me in and locked the door, and then he took off
somewhere—to cool down, so he said...'

'He kept you *prisoner*!' Stephen's raw shock made it
sound as if she had been chained to a dungeon wall and
flogged. 'For how long?'

Kalera adopted a soothingly vague expression as she
accepted a dessert menu from the waiter whose desire
to linger suggested an unprofessional interest in their
intriguing conversation.

'Not long—about an hour or so, I suppose,' she said,
deliberately playing down the drama. She knew exactly
how long it had been. She had been left to stew for
precisely one hour and fifty-one minutes before Duncan
had returned to deliver his pithy lecture on the pitfalls
awaiting gullible young widows who fell prey to
smooth-talking villains.

She looked over the menu, forcing herself to choose
something even though her sweet tooth had been soured
by the subject of their conversation. Stephen's frustration
with the interruption was evident as he selected the
cheeseboard and sent the flapping-eared waiter briskly
on his way before leaning forward again.

'And then what happened?'

Kalera was reluctant to go into too much detail.
Duncan's comments had not been flattering, either to
herself or to Stephen. In fact they had been flagrantly
insulting. She had known that the two men harboured an
intense dislike of each other but until today she hadn't
recognised the true depth of their mutual hostility.

Her efforts to gloss over the worst bits in the retelling

were in vain. For once Stephen seemed insensitive to
her distress, insisting that she describe the abrasive encounter word for word, and wanting to know not only
what Duncan had said, but how he had looked and
sounded when he had realised she would not be cowed
into calling off her engagement.

'And that's all he said about me?' he probed, after she
had informed him that he had been called a low-down,
underhanded, cheating rat; a poor loser who had to compensate for his personal and business inadequacies by
blaming others for his own mistakes; a vain, jealous,
egocentric man who pursued his selfish goals without
caring who he hurt in the process.

'*All!* Isn't that *enough*?' asked Kalera, who had been
humiliated by Duncan's assumption that the only possible reason an attractive man could be interested in her
was because of *him*. And he had the nerve to call
Stephen egocentric! He had even had the gall to hint that
Stephen had tried to cosy up to other female employees
of Labyrinth in the past, but that Kalera was the only
one naive and stupid enough to fall into his honey-trap.

'It's the oldest trick in the industrial espionage book!'
Duncan had declared in disgust. 'Find a lonely, love-
starved female in a sensitive job and seduce her into a
secret affair so that her judgment is so clouded by in-
fatuation she doesn't even notice that her handsome new
lover is pumping her for information...and refuses to
believe it even when she's confronted with cast-iron
proof!'

Smarting from the image of herself as a pathetic emotional accident waiting to happen, Kalera had icily
pointed out that he had produced no proof of anything
other than his own paranoia and, given the fact that his
own judgment was clouded by unreasonable prejudice
against her fiancé, she would thank him to stop making
slanderous remarks unless he was prepared to defend
them in court!

'So, he believes that I only asked you to marry me in order to worm his secrets out of you and to deprive him of your valuable services?' Stephen's aristocratic mouth curled into a contemptuous sneer. 'Did his fertile imagination also suggest a motive for my madness?'

'I thought you asked me here for dinner, not a post-mortem,' Kalera pleaded, his persistence beginning to grate on her nerves. 'Do we have to talk about it any more? I'm just glad it's over and done with, and you must admit it turned out better than we expected. Duncan even apologised for the way he overreacted—said it was just the shock—'

'I'll bet it was a shock!' Stephen laughed grimly. 'Royal doesn't like it when the tables are turned. He likes to be the one to do the shafting. You should have told him where he could stuff his apology and walked out anyway.'

His unaccustomed crudity made her eyes widen. 'Stephen!'

'Well…I don't trust him,' he said, a moody look pushing out his lower lip. 'I just can't believe he wants you to stay on as his secretary when he knows you and I are engaged. *I* wouldn't if our positions were reversed. I wonder what he has up his sleeve? He's a devious swine—I doubt he's doing you any favour by letting you work your notice. He probably intends to make your life hell for the next few weeks. Whatever he pays you it won't be enough…'

It wasn't a matter of money, but of principle and pride, thought Kalera. In the midst of a disarmingly eloquent apology Duncan had somehow extracted a promise from her that she would stay on until the end of the month to help train her successor. She couldn't break her word when Duncan's willingness to keep her on was an act of faith in her integrity; nor did she want to forfeit the respect and liking of her friends at Labyrinth by slinking away from her job as if she were guilty of some wrongdoing.

'I'm sure I can handle it,' she said, hoping that he was wrong. 'I'm tougher than I look, you know.' She straightened her narrow shoulders, laid partially bare by the classic cut of her simple, sleeveless silk sheath. Her slender, breakable body often led people to overlook her inner strength and mistake her serenity for lack of assertiveness.

'I know.' Stephen cupped his hand over hers and gave it a reassuring squeeze. 'I just don't like the idea of you being hurt because of me. I never wanted to put you through this…'

She felt a familiar tightening in her chest followed by a blossoming of sweet contentment, and turned her hand palm up in his grasp, twining her fingers with his. He lifted their clasped hands to his mouth and gallantly saluted her knuckles with a soft kiss.

She loved the way that he could make her feel cherished and special with simple statements of caring rather than extravagant compliments. She recognised the same emotional reserve in him that existed in herself. After Harry was killed so tragically and so young, she hadn't wanted to fall in love again. She hadn't thought that she would ever find another man so perfectly suited to her needs. But then fate had thrown Stephen across her path and his gentle persistence had won her wary heart.

His gaze shifted and suddenly he stiffened, the tender light in his melting brown eyes instantly extinguished. 'Did you tell Royal that we were coming here this evening?'

Kalera raised her finely arched brows at his curtness. Surely Stephen wasn't going to turn paranoid on her too! 'No…at least—I might have mentioned that we were going out to dinner after we shopped for the ring, I suppose, but I don't think I said where. Why?'

'Because he's here—in the restaurant—and he's coming over,' said Stephen through his teeth. 'And you can bet it's not to offer his best wishes.'

Kalera's head snapped around, her fine hair spraying over her silk-clad shoulders as Duncan Royal came to a halt beside her chair. It was only long experience of his eccentric taste in clothes that prevented her mouth from falling open at the sight of his attire. He was dressed from head to toe in black, his sculpted silk velvet jacket cropped like a matador's, the wide lapels and cuffs stiff with flamboyant gold embroidery. Everything about him, from his clothes to the expression on his darkly amused face, reeked of challenge.

'Well, well, well...if it isn't the happy couple,' he drawled, looking down at them with a tigerish smile. 'What an extraordinary coincidence.'

His gaze shifted to their entwined fingers and before Kalera could curb the impulse she had guiltily snatched her hand from Stephen's loosened grasp. She immediately picked up her glass and pretended to be drinking from it, but the glint in Duncan's eye told her that he wasn't fooled.

'Mind if I join you for a while?'

Kalera was rendered speechless by his audacity.

'Yes!'

Ignoring Stephen's violent rejection, Duncan hooked a soft black ankle-boot around the leg of a chair at the next table, abandoned by a foursome for the dance-floor, and dragged it over, not taking his eyes off Kalera's flushed face. He smiled as he positioned the chair too close to hers and sat down, his thigh brushing hers under the round table. She crossed her legs to avoid a repetition and found that it was now her bare arm at risk of being caressed by the plush velvet of his sleeve. His black shirt was figured silk, with covered buttons, she noticed unwillingly. And, dear God...!

'You're wearing an earring!' she gasped, sufficiently

distracted to forget that she had been about to edge her chair away from his.

'Yes, do you like it?' He turned so that the elongated jet and chased gold teardrop swung against the tanned column of his neck, almost brushing the collar of his jacket. A stud or ring was a fairly commonplace declaration of modern macho cool, but the wickedly frivolous elegance of that dangling earring made an entirely different statement. It was the sort of exquisite piece of jewellery that a languid Elizabethan fop might have worn...or a modern rock-and-shock star!

'I didn't even know you had your ear pierced,' murmured Kalera faintly.

'I didn't—until this afternoon,' he said, turning the back of his head towards Stephen and lowering his voice to effectively cut him out of the conversation. 'For some reason I had this sudden, compelling urge to go out and do something just for the sheer hell of it, something satisfyingly primitive, and preferably masochistic... What prompted me to feel like that, do you think, Kalera?'

'I have no idea,' she said, refusing to look into those mocking blue eyes, or acknowledge the gravelly insinuation that she was somehow responsible for his ritual act of self-mutilation. In her experience Duncan needed no outside prompting to encourage his hell-raising impulses. She glanced nervously across the table at Stephen's stony face, and gave him a secret smile in the hope that it might take the sting out of being ignored.

'I know I shouldn't be wearing anything but a stud in it yet,' Duncan went on in his confiding tone, 'but you know me, Kalera, I like to experiment. If you stick to the rules all your life you end up never doing any real *living*.'

His taunt fell on arid ground. Kalera had grown up in a society where there were too few rules rather than too many, and she knew which system she preferred. Duncan, the maverick, was the product of a conventional upper-middle-class upbringing which provided him with the lifelong security of having something to rebel *against*.

He tapped the lobe of his ear, making the earring sway, the polished jet gleaming as it performed its hypnotic little dance in the candlelight.

'So what do you think? Does it suit me?'

Surprisingly it did. The feminine delicacy of the piece presented an exotic contrast to the hard planes of his face and the square jaw shadowed by masculine stubble. But Kalera would die before she admitted it. He was here to cause trouble and she was not going to co-operate by being drawn into his game.

'I think it looks freakish,' said Stephen tightly, the words spilling out from behind his rigid control. 'But then it's typical of you, isn't it, Duncan? Always some outlandish stunt to draw attention to yourself. You'd better be careful: one day people are going to figure out that you're more show than substance.'

'Ever the flatterer, Steve.' Duncan was indifferent to the savage thrust, his interest still squarely centred on Kalera. 'I suppose he's told you how ravishing you look this evening,' he said. His eyes ran over the soft sheen of white silk in a smouldering male appraisal that was completely different from the way he had looked at her that morning. This time his gaze was meant to disturb and arouse and Kalera was grateful for the slight stiffness of the heavy Thai silk which shielded her helpless feminine response to his honeyed blanishment.

It didn't seem to matter that she knew he was mocking her. She could feel her breasts prickling against the cups of her soft lace bra and a dangerous electricity zigzagged through her veins and pooled at the base of her stomach. She unconsciously pressed her thighs together as she kept her expression serene. He didn't have X-ray vision, for goodness' sake; he couldn't possibly know what she was feeling. But the knowing smile kindling in the navy eyes suggested that he could make a far too well educated guess!

'And how very appropriate that you should be wearing the colour of purity and honour,' he drawled, making her pulses spike with renewed apprehension. 'Very bridal...especially with that radiant veil of hair.' He lifted a pale gold lock which had slipped forward to coil on the tablecloth next to her tense elbow and began to curl the silky skein around his finger idly. 'I had no idea it had grown so long. The last time you let your hair down so for me in such glorious abandon it was only halfway down your back, but now it's past your waist...'

Kalera froze, her eyes darting furtively to Stephen, but he appeared so incensed by the sight of Duncan toying with her hair that he failed to notice any hint of collusion in his words.

'What on earth do you think you're doing?' he demanded.

Duncan surveyed the living band of gold that thickly spanned his finger. 'Just admiring your future bride.'

Stephen looked every bit as jumpy as Kalera felt. 'You can do that without pawing at her!'

Duncan's eyes widened insincerely. 'I'm sorry, is that what I was doing, Kalera?'

He slowly unwound the curl and replaced the long tress against the white satin of her bodice, smoothing it back into its former position, seemingly unaware of her sharply indrawn breath as his knuckles skimmed the outer curve of her breast.

'I said, take your hands off her!' hissed Stephen, his face stiff with suppressed anger.

Duncan smiled, all innocence. 'No need to get uptight, Steve. Kalera's not complaining. She's been with me for three years, after all. She's used to me touching her. She knows I'm a very tactile person...'

Stephen disliked the shortened version of his name and Kalera guessed that Duncan knew it and was aiming for maximum provocation with minimum effort. She watched Stephen seethe behind his sophisticated air of self-possession, the closest she had ever seen him to losing his cool.

Duncan had half risen in his seat as he spoke and Kalera let out an inward sigh of relief at the prospect of his departure, but instead of leaving he bent over to heft the bottle from the silver ice-bucket standing on the other side of the table. His mouth kicked up as he read the French label.

'As usual, only the best will do, huh, Steve? Shall I get the waiter to bring another champagne glass so that I can toast your good luck? Better still, let me buy you another bottle to show there's no hard feelings. Give those gossipy old trouts out there a disappointment!'

He sat down again and made a small flourish with his fingers which must have been a pre-arranged signal, for a wine steward immediately came trotting up with a chilled bottle of the same vintage and a third crystal flute.

If his final comment was meant to be a threat, then it worked beautifully to his advantage. Stephen's quick glance around the room told Kalera that, much as he would have liked to reject the offer coldly, he was a hostage to his own good manners. He wasn't going to allow the rest of her evening to be spoiled by allowing them to become embroiled in an unpleasant scene.

They watched as the last of the champagne from the old bottle was poured into Duncan's glass and the new one deftly opened.

'To Kalera...' said the brazen interloper, singing his glass softly against hers and looking deep into the mysterious grey depths of her eyes. 'May you get everything you desire in this world. And to Steve—' He turned, and this time the clash of crystal sounded out like the ring of swords. 'May you get everything you so richly deserve.'

Stephen suddenly seemed impervious to insult, his smile redolent with triumph as he inclined his head.

'Thank you, Duncan. With Kalera as my wife I'm sure I will,' he said smoothly. 'I won't apologise for stealing her away from you because I don't think you appreciated what a quiet gem you had in your possession until she told you she was leaving Labyrinth…for me. You took it for granted that working for the great Duncan Royal must be the most important thing in her life. Well, now you know that it's not—so don't think you can buy her back with a bottle of champagne and a few glib compliments because you can't. She isn't for sale!'

Kalera's hands fluttered in silent protest, aghast at Stephen's unnecessary defence of her integrity. If he was trying to avoid a scene he was definitely going the wrong way about it. Didn't he realise that telling Duncan he couldn't do something was the equivalent of throwing down a gauntlet?

But, instead of responding to the irresistible challenge, Duncan's eyes flickered down, concealing his expression under a thick screen of sable lashes.

'Speaking of gems, I see you're wearing your brand-new engagement ring, Kalera,' was his meek reply. 'May I see?'

She lifted her hand, surprised to find it was clenched into an involuntary fist, and he mimed a silent whistle at the sight of the large diamond solitaire.

'That's quite a rock. A lot bigger than the one Harry gave you, but since love's not measured by the carat I guess that doesn't mean much, does it?'

Stephen was incensed. 'That's an incredibly tasteless and vulgar remark!'

Duncan appeared so remorseful that Kalera knew it was a sham and was horrified by a brief and wholly inappropriate urge to giggle. 'I'm sorry, I know comparisons are odious. It's just that—well, until today Kalera was still wearing Harry's ring and I have difficulty imagining her with another man.' He shook his head reminiscently. 'They were so well matched. I really liked Harry. You never met him, Steve, but he was an all-round nice guy. An incredibly tough act to follow.' He pushed his chair back from the table and stood up.

At last!

'Forgive me, Kalera,' he said, his politeness forcing her to look up into his unconvincingly humble face. 'I'm compounding my sins, aren't I? I didn't mean to upset you by summoning up memories of your first husband, tonight of all nights…'

Liar! He meant to do whatever it took to wreck the romantic mood of their evening. But his plan had back-fired as far as Kalera was concerned, because she knew that Harry would have wanted her to be happy.

So she smiled serenely and murmured that of course she wasn't upset, only to have Duncan give her another lesson in the subtle art of brinkmanship.

'As usual you shame me with your graciousness. But I won't accept that I'm forgiven until you honour me with at least one dance before I go.' He indicated the small, intimate dance-floor occupied by several couples barely moving to the smoochy blues of a small jazz band. 'I doubt that I'll be invited to your wedding so this might be my only chance to dance with the blushing bride. You don't mind, do you, old boy?'

Stephen patently did mind, but Duncan was already stooping to cup Kalera's elbow, applying a secret pres-sure of his fingertips that made her jump to her feet with apparent alacrity, the nerves in her paralysed arm going crazy and tiny pinpoints of white light dancing dizzily in front of her eyes.

Before she could recover from the momentary dis-orientation, Duncan's cunning grip shifted and she found herself propelled into irresistible motion with every ap-pearance of eagerness, leaving Stephen floundering in startled disapproval.

As they moved away from the table Duncan turned his head and asked conversationally, 'Have you told him yet?'

Aware that they weren't fully out of earshot, Kalera stiffened her spine and voluntarily quickened her pace, missing the smirk that Duncan threw over his shoulder.

'Told him what?'

'About us.'

She could feel Stephen's suspicious gaze boring into her back.

'There's nothing to tell!' she denied vehemently.

'No?'

'No!'

They reached the edge of the dance-floor and Duncan swung her lightly into his arms.

'You must lead an astonishingly eventful life if you think that crawling naked into a man's bed and begging him to make love to you is "nothing". Somehow I don't think that Stephen would take the same liberal view. Don't you think he has a right to know that, far from being unappreciative, I'm fully aware of each and every intimate facet of his quiet little gem?'

CHAPTER THREE

THE strength in Kalera's legs melted away and if Duncan hadn't had his arm anchored around her waist she would have sunk ignominiously to the ground. Her long fingernails dug into the soft velvet of his jacket, scrabbling for purchase as she stumbled along, knocking her slender knees against his long legs.

Anyone watching would think that she had never learned to dance, she thought feverishly. But she and Stephen had often danced together and if he was still watching them he would be wondering what on earth was going on. When she went back to the table he would ask what they had been talking about and if she didn't want to create a terrible turmoil in their relationship she would have to lie...

'Oh, *God*!' She moaned, her head wilting towards a gold-embroidered lapel, her temples tightening at the mere thought of the complications that could ensue. An exotic scent teased her nostrils and she dimly recognised the cologne that the staff had given their boss the previous Christmas, and which she had been despatched to select and buy. She had thought the sharp, spicy fragrance with its lingering, sensual undertones might have been designed with Duncan in mind, and now it seemed even more potent, uniquely personalised by the natural musk of his skin.

Duncan's hard palm pressed against her back, bracing the centre of her limp body against his hips as he guided her around the floor in a semblance of grace. His thighs pushed insistently against hers, nudging them into sluggish action, his leading hand tucked close to his shoul-

40

der, keeping her torso nestled against his chest. At six feet four he towered over her, but he was nevertheless surprisingly light on his feet.

'Keep moving. You're doing fine,' he murmured encouragingly, his breath stirring the hair above her ear. 'I won't let you go...'

That was what she was afraid of!

'Why are you doing this?' Her whispery groan trickled out from between pale lips.

'What—dancing?' said Duncan, deliberately misunderstanding her as he deftly side-stepped them past an elderly couple. 'We danced together once before...three years ago, at that party you and Harry gave that first Christmas you worked for me, remember? You and Harry had just moved into a new flat and you invited all your new colleagues from Labyrinth to a house-warming. You didn't expect the boss to turn up too, but I did, and when Harry was dancing with someone else I danced with you—out on the tiny balcony, under the stars, because it was so crowded inside...'

She recognised his technique, having witnessed it often enough in the office. Her head jerked up, away from the illusory comfort of his broad shoulder. 'You're trying to distract me,' she accused, before she realised that perhaps she should be thanking him.

He grinned unrepentantly. 'Is it working?'

'No.' But her feet were beginning to glide more smoothly as she reluctantly recalled the party in question.

She had felt flustered when Duncan had suddenly appeared at the party, alone, when everyone else had brought partners or dates, and she had felt even more uncomfortable during their dance when he had resisted her polite efforts at normal conversation. Having only worked for him for a few weeks, she had attributed his silent abstraction to boredom but now that she knew him well she recognised that he had probably been brooding over a bug in one of his programs, shutting down the rest of his faculties to concentrate his higher-brain function on the problem.

He had held her close that night, too, but so lightly that she hadn't felt trapped or overly aware of the intense masculinity that nowadays she found almost impossible to ignore...

At the time she had also been astonished that Duncan and Harry had hit it off so instantly and so well. They were so radically different from each other...Harry placid and content—some people called him dull—grounded in his strong family values and blessedly ordinary in his dreams and ambitions; and Duncan, the emotional whirlwind, eternally restless and unsatisfied, living life with a greedy enthusiasm that verged on defiance and seemingly incapable of committing himself to any lasting relationship with a woman.

Although Harry had been eight years younger than Duncan, to Kalera he had seemed decades ahead of her boss in maturity. Yet the two men had seemed to connect in some way that she had never quite understood and even though they hadn't seen each other very often they had maintained an easy friendship from which she was excluded, since it largely consisted of Harry trying to teach Duncan how to play golf, a game to which Kalera privately considered her boss was temperamentally unsuited, although as usual he had refused to admit defeat and the intermittent lessons had continued right up until Harry's death.

'That party was the first time I held you in my arms,' Duncan continued, and Kalera suddenly became ultra-conscious of the physical intimacy of their conversation, the way his thigh was sliding between hers as he pivoted their swaying bodies, his solid hips rocking rhythmically against her pelvis. 'And it was all very chaste and innocent, thanks to the fact you were a *very* married woman, but the last time...' He looked down at her, his eyes sultry with secrets, his voice dropping to a throaty purr. 'Eighteen months ago…now, *that* wasn't innocent at *all*…'

'And we both agreed that neither of us would ever mention it again!' she choked, hating the flush that swept across her skin as she averted her face from his. How dared he seek to taunt her with something she had tried so desperately to forget? 'You *promised* that we'd pretend it had never happened—'

'But that's all it ever was, Kalera—a pretence. You and I both know it *did* happen. You can't wipe out the truth simply by ignoring its existence. At the time, I'll admit, it seemed to be the wisest course, but circumstances change…'

'What circumstances?' she asked, trying to pull together her shattered thoughts, furious with herself for letting him catch her off guard.

'Well, now you're no longer a vulnerable, grieving widow, wallowing in guilt over the fact that your sexuality survived your husband's death. If sleeping with Stephen doesn't make you feel like the adulteress, then I guess that lets me off the hook, too—'

Familiar as she was with his love of shock tactics, Kalera still gasped as her eyes whipped up to meet his, her husky voice as icy as her face was hot. 'How *dare* you?'

Her veil of hair flared out as he spun her around in a flamboyant turn, drawing their clasped hands down against his chest to avoid bumping elbows with other dancers. 'As a former lover who was made to feel as if I had scarred you for life, I feel I have a right to a certain interest,' he said piously.

'You and I were *not* lovers,' she corrected him fiercely, her pupils shrinking into tiny pinpoints on ghostly grey backgrounds.

'You're arguing over semantics, Kalera.' He smiled into her angry face. 'We came as close as two people possibly can to making love...the only thing missing was the final act of penetration, which was somewhat superfluous in any case, since we'd both already had the supreme satisfaction of—'

'Duncan!' Kalera's spluttered protest was accompanied by a frantic squeeze of his fingers and a furtive check of the faces in the immediate vicinity, but luckily no one appeared to have overheard his scandalous words.

'I suppose if you *hadn't* had an orgasm you wouldn't have felt so guilty afterwards,' he continued, in defiance of her quietly agonised attempts to hush him. 'You could have persuaded yourself that you endured rather than enjoyed, that I had abused your trust and taken advantage of you, whereas it turned out that *I* was the one being used and abused.'

Somehow she had to stop him from saying those awful, awful things out loud. 'I *wasn't* using you—'

'Not consciously, I'll allow you that, but it seems highly convenient that you didn't decide that what we were doing was wrong until *after* you had everything that you wanted from me. I wonder, would your new lover have been as gracious in the same circumstances?'

'He's not my—' She snapped her teeth shut, appalled at what had almost slipped out.

Navy eyes gleamed like polished silk. 'Good God!' he exclaimed, his voice soft with an infuriating lilt of amused triumph. 'You've agreed to marry the man and you don't even know what he's like in bed? I would have thought Golden Boy would have been anxious to dazzle you with his prowess—'

'Unlike you, Stephen doesn't happen to think that sex is all there is to a relationship!' Kalera tried to quell him with a haughty glare and instead found herself captive to a lambent fire smouldering in his gaze.

'Not *all*—but certainly a large part. You can have lust without love but I don't think a healthy love can exist without a spark of elemental lust and you two don't exactly light up the room with each other,' he murmured. 'Although I suppose if you're marrying for practical reasons rather than love…'

He was fishing and she knew it, but she couldn't help snapping, 'Of course Stephen and I love each other!'

'Do you?' Duncan's scepticism was like sandpaper on her nerves.

'I *have* been in love before,' she said sarcastically. 'I do know what it's like!'

His face seemed to go taut, his eyes narrowing. 'Are you saying that Prior makes you feel the way that Harry did?'

His incredulity gave Kalera the uneasy feeling that she was being backed into a corner she couldn't see. 'Yes—no—' She sounded wishy-washy even to her own ears. 'It's totally different—you wouldn't understand.'

He was not to be so easily dismissed. 'Try me.'

The harshly pitched invitation seemed redolent with deeper meaning. 'I have no intention of discussing it with you—'

'Why? Because Golden Boy wouldn't like it?' he jeered. 'Does he have you so thoroughly under his thumb already, Kalera?'

'No—because I value my privacy,' she corrected him. 'You have no right, whatever was—or was *not*—between us in the past, to try and manipulate me into confiding in you. I've had enough of that kind of thing in my life.' The last tumbled out as something of an afterthought as she looked for their table, trying to catch a reassuring glimpse of Stephen waiting there for her, but even on tiptoe she wasn't tall enough to see over the other dancers blocking her view.

'What do you mean—what confidences has Prior been trying to weasel out of you?' Duncan's dark brows steepened in suspicion, his hand tightening on her lower back. 'I told you that he was operating a hidden agenda.'

Kalera's reference had had nothing to do with Stephen but she was tired of having to defend herself.

'If this is another lecture like this morning's, about my being such an infatuated idiot that I wouldn't notice the bug over the bed for the louse who was in it—you can stop right there!'

He didn't even have the grace to look embarrassed. 'Well, how was I to know that you'd refused to sleep with him? You implied that Boy Wonder had swept you off your feet—and into bed was the obvious assumption!'

'Obvious to *you*, maybe, but thankfully Stephen is more refined. And anyway, I haven't *refused*,' she was unable to resist flinging at him. 'It's just that neither of us wants to rush things. We both happen to be enjoying the process of courtship...'

'I guess sleeping with the enemy while you were still working for me would have been too much like another act of pseudo-adultery,' he said slyly.

Kalera flicked her chin up. 'That had absolutely nothing to do with it!' she declared, wondering how he managed to home in on her doubts with such unerring skill.

'*Absolutely*, huh?' He tilted his head and the outrageous earring danced provocatively in her sight, reminding her how much Duncan loved to flout the conventions, and how successful he was at goading others to forget their polite inhibitions.

'So you don't even feel a teensy-weensy bit unfaithful to me whenever you kiss him?'

She gave him her serene, Mona Lisa smile, while inside she was reeling with shock.

'I don't feel guilty for loving him, if that's what you mean,' she said mildly, and felt proud of her restraint when the mocking light in his eyes abruptly snuffed out. 'I think Harry would have liked him,' she added, intending to put a final period to the conversation.

This time it was Duncan who stumbled as he looked

down at her in amazement, responding with instinctual speed, 'Are you crazy? Harry would have *hated* him.'

'Harry never hated anyone in his life,' she scoffed. His tolerant kindness had been one of the things that she had most loved about her husband.

'Whereas Steve has elevated it to an art form,' said Duncan, recovering his equilibrium and executing a couple of head-spinning turns to prove it. Breathlessly trying to keep up with him, Kalera could feel the frustration that had him almost jumping out of his skin. 'You saw what he was like just now. He was really getting off on the idea of having snatched you out from under my nose—'

As if she were a disputed toy rather than an independent woman with a mind and will of her own!

'You were deliberately trying to provoke him into reacting like that,' she pointed out. 'I'm not going to listen to you run him down just because you don't like him. You're totally unreasonable on the subject of Stephen—'

'*I'm* unreasonable—what about him?'

He sounded like a petulant child and her superior look told him so. 'I suppose the next thing you're going to say is that it isn't fair and it's all his fault,' she said tartly.

He scowled, injecting a note of pathos into his tone that was utterly unconvincing. 'Aren't I even allowed to express a friendly concern for your welfare? I think it's great that you want to get married again, but anyone with half an eye can see that Prior's all wrong for you. You haven't known him very long—I have. Up until a few years ago we were best friends—since our schooldays, in fact—that's how we got into business together...'

Best friends! Kalera kept her face smooth but her clear grey eyes must have clouded with the effort of masking her reaction to the small bombshell for Duncan immediately pounced on her uncertainty.

'Ah...I can see he didn't tell you that—he hates to

admit to his failures…perhaps that's why he never seems willing to learn from his mistakes. Well, it's true; Steve and I know each other a lot better than you seem to think we do. He's always been clever at presenting a good image of himself but underneath all the charm and sophistication he is a serious control freak. He's far too rigid in his thinking for a woman like you. You do realise that he's still on the rebound from his marriage? His divorce only became final a couple of months ago…would that be around about the time that you two met…?'

Kalera refused to dignify the sly insinuation with an answer and he added, 'Has he told you how acrimonious the divorce was, and why he hardly ever sees his son—?'

'Of course he has,' she interrupted tightly. She wasn't going to let him frighten her with lurid tales of Stephen's broken marriage. Thanks to her upbringing she had a deep respect for people's right to keep their thoughts and feelings private. At the various communes which her free-spirited parents had inhabited, there had never been any real personal privacy, either physically or psychologically, and young Kalera had grown to loathe the ubiquitous group meetings endemic to such places, where everyone was expected to expose their most intimate secrets in the interests of universal 'truth' and self-enlightenment. Cruel opinions and petty spite were praised for their 'honesty' while those who had no emotional dramas to enact were criticised for 'holding back' by repressing their true feelings.

Kalera thought a little repression would have been healthier for all concerned. She didn't want or expect to know everything that had gone on in Stephen's past life, just as certain areas of her own past were closed off to him. She certainly didn't expect him to be perfect. The fact that he still couldn't forgive his ex-wife for the affair that had destroyed their marriage was understandable—

he was a proud man who possessed a touchingly old-fashioned code of morals. She hadn't met six-year-old Michael as yet, because his mother's vengeful bitterness over the divorce proceedings was such that, for the sake of his son's emotional well-being, Stephen had felt it advisable not to insist on exercising his visitation rights under the custody agreement. But Kalera was confident that she would be able to befriend the boy when the time came for the visits to resume.

'If there's anything else I need to know, I'd rather find it out from Stephen, thank you very much,' she said, to forestall any more tale-bearing.

Her stubborn loyalty caught Duncan on the raw. 'Dammit, Kalera,' he exploded. 'I'm only trying to help!'

'Yes—to help make trouble between Stephen and I so you won't have to suffer the inconvenience of training another secretary to withstand your tantrums!' she blurted out.

Duncan stopped dead, ignoring the couples who cannoned into them. 'Is *that* what you think this is about?' he growled.

'Well, isn't it?'

An unholy expression crossed his face and Kalera hastily decided that her question could remain safely rhetorical. Arching her upper body away from him, she gingerly tested his grip by pushing lightly against his chest. The broad, flat plane vibrated beneath her palms, the thin silk of his shirt no barrier to the throb of his vital life force. Her own pulse accelerated in response to the quick, hard beat and she fought to quell her unruly awareness. 'Uh—maybe we should go back to the table now—I'm sure my dessert must have turned up by now...'

'Not sweet enough, Kalera?' He purred the sickly cliché, his arm sliding more securely around her waist as his torso tracked hers. 'I beg to differ; if anything your problem is that you're *too* sweet. But by all means let's continue our little chat in front of Stephen—I'm sure he'd be fascinated…'

He bent one knee and Kalera suddenly found herself in a deep dip, arched over his arm in a classic posture of feminine submissiveness, her hair almost sweeping the floor. For an instant she felt as if she was falling through time and space, her only connection to reality a pair of smouldering blue eyes that challenged her to enjoy the ride. A few chuckles tinkled in her burning ears, confirmation—had she needed it—of the exhibition they were making of themselves.

'Kind of makes you think of the phrase "it takes two to tango", doesn't it?' Duncan murmured, his back taking the strain of their combined weight as he slowly eased them both upright again. He raised his eyebrows at her delicately flushed face. 'So…do you really want to involve Stephen, or should we just keep dancing while we settle our unfinished business?'

Kalera bit her lip. As far as she was concerned there was nothing to settle, but Duncan in this dangerously volatile mood was impossible to predict. If she attempted to thwart him, heaven knew what mischief his fertile brain might hatch.

'He'll be wondering where I am…'

His shrug was magnificently uncaring. 'He knows you're with me.'

'Precisely.'

Her arid reply made him chuckle in rich delight. He threw back his head, the sable hair blending invisibly into his collar as he closed his eyes and began to move to the music again, drawing her into the sinuous, syncopated rhythm as if she were an extension of his own body. Both his arms were now loosely linked around her waist and, looking up at his darkly attractive face, Kalera was struck by a shivery premonition of disaster.

'You wouldn't really, would you?' she murmured,

tearing her eyes away from his narrow mouth before she was tempted to wonder whether he would taste the same, or whether, like a superior vintage, he had matured with age...

His eyelids flickered but didn't lift. 'Wouldn't really what?'

Her husky voice was even deeper than usual. 'You implied you were going to tell Stephen about what we— about what happened.'

'No—I said I thought he ought to know.'

Her fingers pleated the black silk shirt-front in an unconscious attitude of pleading. 'Why? Because you want to hurt him? If this is to do with an old quarrel between you and Stephen, why can't you leave me out of the argument?'

'Because you, my dear, have planted yourself firmly in the middle of it.'

Exasperation conquered her desire to appease. 'I am *not* your dear!'

'Not for want of trying.' His eyes opened to mere slits of glittering wickedness. 'But no...I suppose you're right; in bed it was *darling* that you begged me to call you—'

'That was a long time ago,' she gritted, the endearment short-circuiting her memory banks, throwing out a shower of white-hot sparks which coalesced into the haunting spectre of a man in the throes of violent passion, his thick, straining limbs gleaming like polished teak against rumpled white sheets...

'Eighteen months, two weeks and three days and—' he tilted their entwined hands so he could look at the jewelled gold watch strapped to his wrist '—eleven hours...*darling*.'

Oh, God, he remembered the exact date, even the precise *time*, for goodness' sake! And all this time she had thought that *she* was the only one to be cursed with perfect recall of her fall from grace...

It had been a very bad day; the culmination of a long string of bad days. Her family and friends had been enormously kind immediately after Harry's death but as the months crawled by they had all moved on with their own lives and expected practical, down-to-earth Kalera to buckle down and do the same. She had done her best to justify everyone's confidence in her ability to 'get over' the awful tragedy that had shattered her life, reasoning that eventually the calm acceptance that she was projecting would become a reality. But the opposite had proved true and the serene façade had become increasingly fragile. She'd felt hollow inside, scoured out by an awful sense of helplessness that rendered her horribly vulnerable to the loneliness that constantly ached in the marrow of her bones.

For a whole six months she had managed to convince herself and everyone else that she was coping magnificently well and then the whole fragile edifice had crashed to the ground—over something as ridiculous as a simple typing error.

It had been late one afternoon and Duncan had called her into his office to query some missing words in a confidential memo which completely altered his intended meaning. In typically extravagant fashion he'd gone on to proclaim that her fetish for editing his colourful language was in danger of ruining his business, that she was turning his correspondence into drab, grey, conformist tracts which were boring his clients into questioning his creativity.

In the middle of this silly piece of teasing Kalera had horrified them both by bursting into tears, and Duncan had practically leapt over the desk to get to her before she could flee for a dark corner in which to hide her embarrassing attack of emotion.

'I know, I know...I miss Harry too,' he said hoarsely, sweeping her shuddering body against his large frame, devastating her with his instant empathy and willingness to tackle the subject that everyone else had been tactfully avoiding. 'It still hurts, doesn't it, baby? You can tell me. You just cry it all out...'

She had no choice; once started, the flood of grief was impossible to stop. All the horror, all the fear, all the anguish of the day that Harry died came pouring out as Duncan sat beside her on his couch, alternately patting her back and warming her cold hands between his, dabbing at her soggy face with his brightly checked handkerchief and doing far more good with his vague, nonsensical murmurs than had the intrusively helpful woman from Victim Support or the bland psychologist paid for by the Accident Compensation Commission.

Not that there had been anything accidental about Harry's death. She still found it difficult to believe that her quiet, modest, slow-talking, unadventurous husband had died a national hero.

He and Kalera had been lunching at a peaceful, open-air tourist spot when a madman had started spraying gunfire, killing five and wounding a dozen others, including several children. While panic-stricken patrons had cowered behind flimsy wooden tables or attempted to flee the chaos of blood and screams, Harry had launched himself into the firing line to protect a mother and her baby daughter, saving their lives at the cost of his own.

Bleeding from a massive chest wound, he had somehow still found the strength to grab the barrel of the gun as the blank-eyed gunman stepped up to deliver the *coup de grâce*, and the police psychiatrist had speculated afterwards that perhaps Harry's action had jolted the man out of his automaton-like state long enough to realise that there could be only one escape from the consequences of his actions, for he had suddenly turned his weapon on himself, ending his murderous spree with a bullet to the brain.

It had all happened so fast that there had barely been

time to react and yet as Kalera had crawled out from behind the metal rubbish drum where she and Harry had taken cover time had seemed to slow almost to a stop, her movements seeming painfully sluggish and ineffectual as she'd frantically pushed at the dead gunman's heavy body in an effort to free her husband from its macabre embrace. In what had seemed like an interminable wait for the police and emergency services to arrive, Harry's life-blood had gushed through her fingers and soaked into the gravel on which he was sprawled. In typical fashion he had whispered to her not to worry and in the ambulance on the way to the hospital she had watched helplessly as the life quietly leaked out of his torn body, had leaned over him and smiled into his rapidly clouding eyes, talking desperately about the future even as she felt an ominous clenching in her lower abdomen.

Harry had lapsed into unconsciousness and died before they reached the hospital...died believing that at least part of him would live on in the long-awaited child that nestled in her womb. To Kalera it seemed bitterly ironic that she'd survived the vicious hail of bullets without a physical scratch, only to miscarry her baby two days later. A coincidence, the doctor had assured her, but she'd chosen to add the loss of her tiny daughter to the list of the gunman's victims. It was easier to accept that the miscarriage had been caused by trauma and stress than by the fact that the precious life that she and Harry had conceived out of their love might have been too flawed to survive.

Sometimes, in her darkest hours, she even blamed her husband for his fatal act of heroism, for choosing to abandon those he loved to protect two total strangers.

'Why? Why did he have to play the hero like that?' she had sobbed into Duncan's chest.

'He wasn't playing, he was just being true to himself.' The deep voice rumbling in her ear was for once calm and measured. 'Guys like Harry—decent, compassionate men who hate to see other people hurt and have the courage to act on their convictions—are life's real heroes, you know, not the macho, aggressive, fearless warriors that you see glorified in big-budget action movies. What he did was instinctive to his nature—he was trying to help someone more vulnerable than himself.'

'But what about *me*?' It was a bewildered cry of angry betrayal. 'He left *me* alone, and I was his *wife*…I was vulnerable too!' Her hand clenched unknowingly over her empty womb. 'He had nothing to defend himself with—how did he expect to stop a man with a gun?'

Duncan swallowed her cold fist in his warm grip, prising it away from her stomach to rest against his reassuringly solid breastbone. 'He must have believed you were safe where you were—out of sight, whereas that young woman was right there in the killer's path, struggling to get her baby out of her broken push-chair. You said there was no time to think, so Harry wasn't worrying about consequences, he was just reacting to his gut feelings…'

'All I felt was fear. I froze up—' She choked, her head sinking with shame as she remembered how she had shivered at Harry's side as they had crouched behind the painted bin.

A forceful hand cupped her delicate jaw, lifting her tear-streaked face so that she was looking directly into dark blue eyes ablaze with a fierce emotion that was startling in its intensity.

'I'm glad you did. It probably saved your life. If you'd followed Harry you would have been shot too. You might have died, or been badly maimed like some of the others. Don't expect me to be anything but grateful that it didn't happen.'

His palm shaped her pale cheek, his fingertips resting on the throbbing pulse at her temple, making her vividly aware of the life that coursed through her veins. No, she hadn't wanted to die, and she didn't regret surviving, being whole…

'But I should have tried to stop him,' she whispered. 'One moment he was beside me, the next he was gone. I could have stopped him…'

'You had no control over the situation at the time and you can't assume it in hindsight. There was nothing you could have done, Kalera, and no amount of torturing yourself over futile what ifs is going to change that fact. Only one person is responsible for what happened that day.'

'He deserved to die,' she grated bitterly, still unwilling and unable to feel any compassion for the man whose refusal to take medication for his depressive illness had resulted in such senseless carnage. 'Harry didn't.'

'No.'

Braced for a response that preached the healing qualities of forgiveness, Duncan's simple acknowledgement of her right to bitterness reopened the floodgates.

'Today would have been our sixth wedding anniversary,' she admitted in a wobbly voice as the tears dripped down her face, gathering in the V-shaped dam formed by the web of his thumb and forefinger and spilling over the back of his hand.

'Ah, Kalera…' There was a wealth of understanding in his voice as he bent to rest his forehead against hers, rolling it slowly back and forth, ironing out her crumpled brow. 'No wonder you're feeling so alone…'

'And tomorrow—tomorrow is the day that my baby was due to be born,' she wept, abandoning herself to his sheltering strength.

Duncan was the only other person at work who had known about her pregnancy—something that he had guessed for himself even before her suspicions were medically confirmed. Dismayed by the acuteness of his perception, she had reason to be grateful that he had respected her plea not to mention her condition to anyone else, for it was barely two weeks later that tragedy had struck—two weeks during which she and Harry had hugged their secret joy to themselves, savouring the fact that they were to become parents at last.

The loss of her unborn child had been such a deeply personal grief that Kalera had been unwilling to expose it to the harsh glare of publicity which had surrounded Harry's death and subsequent funeral. Her parents had chided her for dropping out of the grief therapy provided for the surviving victims of the massacre but the gruelling sessions had reminded Kalera too uncomfortably of the mind-games played by the so-called spiritual gurus of her youth.

Shivering in Duncan's arms, she finally acknowledged that she couldn't escape her pain by pretending it didn't exist; she was merely prolonging the agony of her bereavement. But she was terribly afraid that the feelings of guilt and abandonment which she was experiencing would *never* go away...

When Kalera's tears had finally dwindled into shuddering sniffles, Duncan tucked his handkerchief into her hand and hoisted her from the couch.

'Come on, I'm taking you home—'

'No, really—I'll be all right,' she protested automatically, brushing the back of her hand across her swollen eyelids.

'No, you won't—you look terrible,' said Duncan ruthlessly. 'As if you've been beaten with a rubber hose.'

It was precisely how she felt—fragile and pulpy, inside and out. Every bone seemed to be bruised to the marrow and her head felt stuffed with cotton wool.

'Anyway, it wasn't a suggestion, it was an order. We're both finishing early for the day.'

Unprecedented orders from a self-acknowledged workaholic. 'But—you've got a meeting in twenty minutes—' she protested weakly.

'So? I'll tell Anna to reschedule. Get your things and

we'll slip out the back way before anyone knows we're gone.' He was tapping out a message to Anna on his keyboard even as he spoke and, exhausted by emotion, Kalera allowed herself to be whisked out of the office and into his little-used private lift.

At that moment she would have meekly followed Duncan Royal into the jaws of hell.

Instead he turned out to be her guide, and helter-skelter ride, to a brief slice of heaven.

CHAPTER FOUR

ONCE down in the underground car park a firm hand in the small of her back steered Kalera towards the red McLaren F1 that was Duncan's most spectacular extravagance.

'But what about my car?' she fretted belatedly, glancing over her shoulder at the sedate family saloon which Harry had always kept in immaculate condition.

'It'll be safe enough here overnight. If you think I'm going to let you drive in the state you're in, you've got another think coming,' Duncan said, handing her into the passenger seat of his car and brushing aside her fumbling fingers to buckle her into the safety harness and tuck her skirt under her slender thigh, the gentleness of his touch a direct contrast to the sternness of his words.

Kalera's reserves of energy were too low to generate even a token objection to his high-handedness. She shut her mind to the difficulties of getting to work the next day and sank into the plush leather, closing her eyes and allowing the deep, throaty purr of the powerful engine to act like a sedative on her tired brain.

To her relief Duncan made no effort to engage her in conversation and, instead of surging onto the streets with his usual impatience, drove with an exaggerated care that she realised with detached amusement was a positive insult to the rampant machine under his control.

Insulated by her weary lassitude, Kalera wasn't prepared for the icy attack of panic that hit her when she opened her eyes and saw the signpost for her street.

'No! Wait—don't turn here—' She flung out a hand, clutching at the flowing sleeve of Duncan's loose-fitting

white shirt, urgently tugging his arm away from the
wheel, causing the car to shy like a nervous thorough-
bred.

Duncan cursed violently under his breath as he
braked, skilfully controlling their sudden swerve. 'Why?
This is where you live…'

Only because Harry's life insurance had paid off the
hefty mortgage, otherwise Kalera wouldn't have been
able to continue to afford the payments on her single
income. She could see the green roof of the house which
they had saved so hard to buy…a family home in a
suburban neighbourhood bustling with children, within
walking distance of the local shops and primary school.
A house purchased on hope and dreams…

Kalera's breath caught in her throat, her restraining
grip tightening, her skin creeping with an inexplicable
dread. 'I don't want to go home yet!' she declared flatly.

Duncan pulled into the kerb and looked down at her
tense white face.

'I wasn't just going to dump you on the doorstep and
run, Kalera,' he said, disentangling his crumpled shirt
from her stiff fingers. 'You won't have to be by yourself—I'll come inside with you—'

'No!' She shuddered, unable to articulate her nameless
fear. He thought the house was empty, but it wasn't.
Memories crouched in the very walls, waiting to leap
out at her the moment she let her guard down. 'No! I
don't want to go in there. Please—can't we go somewhere else?'

'Where would you like me to take you?'

'I don't know—it doesn't matter…anywhere!' she
said, her voice rising shrilly. 'I don't care—please—
can't you just *drive*?'

That was how she had ended up at Duncan's home
and, ultimately, in his bed.

Some of the details were a blur. For instance she
didn't remember the drive to his house in Ponsonby, and

only vaguely recalled the cup of sweet tea and sugary snack that he had forced her to eat in his aggressively modern kitchen when he had discovered that she had skipped lunch. She did remember the blooming headache that had made her grateful to accept his offer of a lie-down in a cool, mint-green room with a soft-sprung bed and dark teak shutters with which she could shut out the strident afternoon sun. Sleep was the perfect escape, both from her own pain and the subtle pressure of Duncan's curiosity.

When she woke up it was pitch-dark, and she was sweating and trembling violently from a familiar nightmare, her throat dry and raw, her legs cramping as if she had been running too fast for too long. Except for her shoes she was still fully dressed and her twisted clothes stuck clammily to her skin as she fought free of the light blanket that had been placed over her as she slept.

She groped her way off the bed, her heart hammering as she tried to orientate herself in the smothering darkness. She knocked against something with sharp edges and cried out as she fell and suddenly Duncan was there, picking her up and setting her back on her unsteady feet.

'Kalera? Are you all right? I heard you shouting something.'

'I...woke up,' she said stupidly, her heart easing its frantic beat as she recognised the harsh, rasping tone. She stepped away from his touch. 'I—for a moment I didn't know where I was. Wh-what time is it?'

'Late.' There was a whisper of sound and a wall-light clicked on, and she found herself blinking at a dishevelled-looking Duncan, his jaw roughened with dark whiskers, his hair lightly matted on one side of his head, a faint pink crease-mark impressed on his hard cheek. A short black towelling robe was insecurely belted at his waist, the sagging lapels revealing a silky swatch of dark hair curling across his deep chest.

'Too late for you to bother going home.' His voice

was blurred around the edges with sleep but his eyes
were sharp and alert as he watched her fold her arms
around her waist in an unconscious gesture of self-
protection, her gaze jerking away from his bared chest.
'When you didn't wake up for dinner I thought you'd
probably sleep through until the morning.'

Her arms tightened about her waist as she looked enviously at the bed, wishing that oblivion were as easy
as he made it sound. She rarely had an unbroken night's
sleep these days.

'You may as well go back to bed for what's left of
the night,' he added softly, persuasively. 'My room is
just across the hall if you need me—near enough to hear
you call out. You know nothing can happen to you here.'

Her tautly strung nerves quivered. Didn't he realise
that it was when you felt most safe that you were most
vulnerable? Innocent places and activities could harbour
a danger all the more horrific for being so unexpected.

When Kalera didn't answer immediately, his voice
roughened. 'Do you want me to get dressed and get the
car out?'

He would do it, too, if she said yes. He made her feel
both guilty and foolish with the gruff offer. She couldn't
be so churlish as to accept.

'No.' It came out as a husky whisper and she tried
again. 'No, you don't have to do that...but I—' Her
hands plucked distastefully at her crumpled grey suit and
high-necked maroon blouse, more suited to an air-
conditioned office than a warm spring night. 'I feel so
hot and sticky—I'm not used to sleeping in my
clothes... I suppose that's what woke me up.'

He didn't point out that people didn't usually wake
up screaming from the heat.

'There's a bathroom next door; a warm shower might
make it easier for you to get back to sleep. I always have
one before I go to bed.' And before she could begin to
feel uneasy at the thought of taking her clothes off in

his domain Duncan yawned hugely, stretching his arms so that his robe sagged even more, sliding off one sleek, muscled shoulder. 'I put a clean towel and some things in there for you earlier. Meantime you won't mind if I turn in…I'm definitely not very scintillating company this early in the morning. G'night, Kalera.'

He turned and shuffled out of the room in a manner that suggested his brain had already checked the close-box on the window of his consciousness.

The 'things' he had left in the bathroom were neatly arranged on the top of a folded bath sheet, hand-towel and face-cloth—shampoo and a fragrant feminine soap pristine in its wrapper, a toothbrush still in its packet and a black silk pyjama top with a monogrammed 'R' on the pocket.

Kalera used the toothbrush and then, ignoring the shampoo, wrapped her hair in the hand-towel while she stood under the warm, pulsing water. The clear red soap slicked over her smooth skin, the bubbles bursting in a strawberry-scented flurry that made her sharply aware of how long it was since she had bought anything but util-itarian supermarket toiletries. Since Harry died she had avoided anything that served to emphasise her feminin-ity. To want to feel attractive or sexy seemed a betrayal of their love.

She lifted her face to the spray, helpless to prevent the insidiously arousing memories that were suddenly swirling around her, like the rising steam in the small glass cubicle. Harry had loved to join her in the shower. Her dear staid, stodgy husband had been a secret sen-sualist and anything but stodgy in his lovemaking. It was through his unashamed delight in the physical side of their relationship that Kalera had learned to revel in her own deeply sensual nature.

From the time she was old enough to realise what her parents' 'open marriage' really meant she had nurtured a strong distaste for casual promiscuity. Unlike the rest of her schoolfriends' parents, Kris and Silver Donovan had *expected* their daughter openly to indulge her adolescent sexual curiosity and had been bewildered when she'd shown no interest in exercising her freedom. But Kalera had yearned for a conventional morality where sex was cherished as something special—personal and private between two people, not just another physical appetite to be satisfied with whomever happened to be convenient and willing. She'd been wary of the strong passions that seethed through her maturing body, repressing her sexual urges out of fear that she was destined to roam in her intemperate mother's footsteps.

It was Harry who had freed her from her inhibitions. He had shown her that enjoying sex with the man she loved didn't mean she had a predisposition for promiscuity, that it was possible to be wild and out of control in bed and still be utterly faithful out of it. After Harry she had never looked at another man, never been tempted, not even in her fantasies.

As her hands moved over her soapy skin Kalera ached for her husband's slow touch, for the obliterating pleasure that could block out everything but the moment. She missed the physical side of their relationship with a fierceness that shocked and dismayed her—it seemed so selfish to be dwelling on what *she* had lost, when it was Harry who had lost everything…

Her eyes closed as her palms glided up over her slim hips and supple waist and cupped her firm, high breasts, shaping them with yearning fingers. She imagined that she had Harry back, that he was right there behind her, that they were *his* hands slipping and sliding erotically over the slick, wet hills and valleys of her flesh…

She groaned, the involuntary sound jolting her out of her forbidden fantasy into a horrified awareness of what she was doing. Her hands shook as she hurriedly turned off the shower and grabbed the fluffy bath sheet, quickly towelling the moisture off her tingling skin.

Her whole body felt tight and hot and achy, and a treacherous weakness trembled in her limbs. Avoiding her image in the steamy mirror, she unwrapped the towel from her head and shook out the loose pins from her sagging hairstyle, raking her fingers through the tangles. She shrugged into the pyjama jacket, shivering as the cool silk settled against her sensitised skin, and rolled up the too long sleeves, but when it came to the elegantly small buttons the fine tremor in her fingers made her so clumsy that she gave up, wrapping the slithery fabric across her front and folding her arms under her breasts to keep it in place. The jacket, designed to be roomy on a tall, muscular male, swamped her in loose folds to below her knees—like a black shroud, she thought with sudden revulsion.

From outside in the quiet street came several short, sharp reports as a cranky car sputtered past with a backfiring engine. The small explosions echoed like gunshots in Kalera's overwrought mind and her mouth flooded with the metallic taste of terror as she was catapulted back into her worst nightmare.

Half crouching in an instinctive effort to make herself as small and insignificant a target as possible, she darted blindly for sanctuary. The door to Duncan's bedroom was ajar but the interior was dark and silent and she faltered, her ears straining for the reassuring sound of his presence, but she was unable to distinguish anything over the violent pounding of her pulse.

He had promised he would be there if she needed him. He had to be there! Her panic-stricken sense of disorientation was fading, but fear clogged like pack-ice in her veins as logic battled with her unreasoning dread of abandonment. If Duncan was only asleep, surely she should be able to hear the sound of his breathing? Oh, God! Even young, apparently healthy people sometimes died of heart attacks, or suddenly, in their sleep, for no reason...

She pushed the door wide, the muted light from the hall projecting her blurry shadow across the pale carpet as she crept into the room. She could see a motionless lump in the centre of the wide bed and a thready whimper escaped her lips, her heart stopped momentarily, only to resume its frantic beat as Duncan abruptly reared up on one elbow, his reactive speed indicating that he had been lying there awake in the dark.

'Kalera? What's wrong?'

Unutterable relief throttled her speech. Nothing was wrong. Not now. In the dim light she could see that Duncan was bare-chested, his broad shoulders gleaming like polished wood, the muscles of his supporting arm bulging in a manner that proclaimed him strong and vigorous and pumping with life. She had never looked at Duncan as a *man* before and now suddenly there he was—blatantly, inescapably, irrefutably male, a potent symbol of the passion that had been wiped out of her life by a bitter stroke of fate.

'Can't you go back to sleep?' He pushed himself further upright and the sheet slid down his ridged abdomen to pool across his lap.

Kalera moistened her lips and shook her head, her hair streaming down her back, her anchoring clutch on the pyjama top falling away as she stepped towards the bed, driven by a compulsion she couldn't deny. The unbuttoned jacket gaped, displaying a wide strip of pale flesh from the pulsing hollow in her throat to the soft shadow of fluff at the base of her belly.

Duncan's shoulders went rigid with disbelief, his eyes glinting in the darkness as he wrenched them back up to her face.

'My God, Kalera—what are you doing?' His deep voice was hoarse with shock as she shrugged her shoulders and the black garment whispered to the floor in a slither of silk.

Silhouetted against the light from the hall, she looked

as slim as a boy, but as she scrambled onto the high bed the tilt and flex of her body revealed the tantalising sway of sweetly rounded breasts tipped with dark, pointed nipples and the feminine curve of her bottom.

'I'm cold,' she said truthfully, burrowing under the covers until her body collided with his, the burning heat of her skin making nonsense of her words as she slid her arms around his rigid torso, tugging until he collapsed back onto the white pillows. 'Hold me... please...I need someone to hold me, to make me warm again...'

She tangled her legs in his and nuzzled her face into his hairy chest, inhaling the aroma of clean, healthy male. She had wondered if he was wearing anything under the bedclothes and now her curiosity was searingly satisfied. His big, nude body was a patchwork of deliciously contrasting textures and tiny thrills of anticipated ecstasy shivered across her skin as she measured herself boldly against his rigid length. Her parted lips brushed one of his flat nipples and he groaned, his hands gripping her upper arms as he tried to hold her squirming body discreetly at bay.

'For God's sake, Kalera—'

She arched her back, rolling her pelvis against the broad saddle of his hips, and revelled in the hot thrust of desire he was unable to hide, a glorious reaffirmation of his life-giving potency. An answering response rippled through her empty womb, flooding her with bitter-sweet yearning.

'Oh, yes...that feels so good, so hot...' she murmured eagerly, pushing her smooth thigh between his legs, twisting her upper body so that her stiff nipples scraped against his chest and her hip angled across the thickening shaft of flesh stirring against his belly. He uttered another tormented groan.

'No, we can't do this—'

But even as he spoke his hands were shifting to cage

her ribs, his thumbs angling into the crease under her soft breasts, pushing them up into pouting prominence, his thighs clenching around hers, a sheen of perspiration slicking across his skin.

'Yes, we can,' she said huskily, sinking her teeth into his heaving chest and sucking at the tiny wound, the epitome of the sultry temptress.

He growled deep in his throat and slammed her over onto her back. 'Dammit, Kalera, can't you see I'm trying to be noble here?' he said thickly.

He had kicked the bedclothes astray in the flurry of motion and in the strip of light that fell across the bed Kalera could see something far more fascinating than his nobility. The lower half of his body was as hard-packed with muscle as his upper half and the heavy arousal springing from the thick cloud of jet-black hair in his groin was equally splendid. She wanted to absorb the very essence of that strength and splendour into her body, to make it part of herself. The very last thing she required from him tonight was gentlemanly consideration and restraint. He couldn't reject her, he *mustn't*...!

'Please...' She reached down between them to capture him in an intimate caress. 'I need you to make love to me...'

His whole body jerked, the breath hissing between his clenched teeth as he felt her slim fingers wrap themselves around his swollen shaft. 'It's not me you really want,' he gritted in a last-ditch effort to shock her back to sanity. 'It's Harry—'

'But I can't have Harry,' she pointed out, her grey eyes stormy with thwarted passion as she met his tortured gaze. 'So why shouldn't I have *this*...?'

Her eyes fell as her thumb stroked across the moist tip of satin-sheathed steel that was the proof of his desire. She watched him pulse helplessly within her snug fist. 'So full of life,' she husked enviously, teasing him with another slow caress. 'I want to taste it, touch it, feel it hot and strong inside me, filling me up until I can't think, only *feel*...'

'Dear God!' Duncan shuddered, his noble intentions crumbling under the erotic assault. He plunged his hands into her shimmering hair as she would have bent her head to follow her words with her mouth, locking his fingers around the back of her skull and tilting the pale oval of her face up for his savage appraisal. He looked deep into her eyes, seeing past the hectic glaze of desire to the heart of her desperation. 'All right, damn you! If sex is your drug of choice, then I'll be your fix. But we do this *my* way, Kalera—'

'Call me darling,' she interrupted feverishly, too exulted by her victory to care about the terms of his surrender. 'We don't need names or labels. For tonight, let's just be a man and a woman...' Names would make everything too real, would disrupt her lovely fantasy...

An angry spark smouldered in Duncan's shadow-masked eyes, warning Kalera that he guessed what she was trying to do, but instead of arguing the insult to his ego his mouth kicked into a dangerous curve, his aggressive self-confidence rising flamboyantly to the challenge.

'Darling...' he purred obediently, the predatory nature of his smile anything but submissive. He slowly began moving his hips, pushing himself against her soft palm, maintaining the delicious friction as he rolled onto his side and stroked his hands slowly down her throat and over her body from breasts to belly and back to her breasts again, fondling the taut peaks until she begged mindlessly for his mouth.

He complied instantly with her greedy demand, bending his head to rub his face against the soft pillows of milky flesh, the slight sandiness of his smooth-shaven jaw an erotic contrast to the silken glide of his cheek and the warm, wet whip of his tongue as he traced around each velvety areola, drawing them into the cavern of his mouth, nibbling and sucking at her dusky nipples until they were glistening peaks of swollen ripeness, as tight and hard as the exquisite knot of tension that budded in the secret folds between her restless legs.

'Yes, oh, yes…' Her voice throbbed with relief as he stroked her there too, insinuating his hand between her silky thighs and dipping his fingers into the damp, creamy heat, parting the moist petals and finding the most sensitive spot on her body with a tantalising skill that made her almost burst with unbearable delight.

'Do you like that, darling?' he murmured against her dewy breast, moving his invading fingers deeper into her receptive body. 'Tell me…tell me everything you want and I'll give it to you…'

But Kalera could no longer form her thoughts into a coherent pattern of words. Sweet, hot chills shivered over her skin as she threshed against the sheets, her fingernails digging into Duncan's back, raking across the straining muscles as she plunged into a world of pure sensation unadulterated by fear or shame—a place where there was no evil, no pain, no smothering survivor's guilt, only a soaring lust for life celebrated in the most elemental human way. The raw sexuality of the sleek and powerful lover she had summoned out of the depths of her loneliness triggered a primitive mating response that swept away her inhibitions, his ruthless dedication to servicing her every sensual whim encouraging her to become more and more reckless in her demands.

But Duncan was in no hurry. He lingered over the bone-melting caresses, feeding her wild craving by offering tiny tastes of the promised fulfilment and inviting her to match him stroke for stroke. Every time that Kalera's eyes drifted closed in order to concentrate on her turbulent desire he would pause until she opened them again, forcing her to watch what they were doing to each other, to share with him each and every moment of voluptuous pleasure as it registered in her expressive grey eyes. His own eyes glittered with fierce triumph as he controlled her passionate frenzy, channelling and refining it into an exquisite mutual torture. Again and again he drove her close to the pinnacle of release with his hands and mouth, imprinting his identity on her mind and body, bombarding her with sensations so intense that she barely registered his subtle resistance to her efforts to take him into her body.

But eventually, as the tension inside her built relentlessly towards yet another unattainable peak, Kalera's frustration exploded into open rebellion. It wasn't enough. Underlying the pleasure there was still the painful sense of anxiety, of emptiness that only he could fill.

'More...I want more,' she panted, writhing beneath the heavy crush of his body, clamping her legs around his lean hips and arching her spine as her hand snaked down to try to force his bluntly engorged flesh into the slick folds of her womanhood, her guiding hand clumsy with impatience.

'Wait—'

He was huge and hard, blatantly ready for her, and she couldn't understand why he was holding back. 'No...love me now... Please—I need you to come inside me *now*!'

His big body surged and trembled, a guttural sound tearing from his chest. Sensing that he was at the limit of his self-control, Kalera whispered more needy, greedy sex words as she waited, swooning for the first, deep, delicious, driving thrust that would simultaneously heal and splinter her asunder. But again he eluded her, this time with a finality that was flatteringly—and shatteringly—simple.

'Oh!' The silky wetness that flowed over her fingers stunned Kalera into stillness as convulsive shudders ripped through Duncan's body, his groan of completion muffled in the curve of her throat.

'*Oh!*' Tears of anger and bitter disappointment stung

her eyes as she felt a deep laxity ripple up his spine, mocking the excruciating tension in her strung-out body. His skin was damp with perspiration, and the musky scent of his sexual satisfaction was an added insult to her simmering frustration. 'You…you—' Her voice broke on a half-sob as she struggled to control her chagrin.

'Kalera…' His ragged plea for understanding held a hint of rueful amusement that turned her bewilderment to stinging resentment. She felt angry, deprived…

'Get off me!' she choked, trying to wedge her elbows against his heaving chest so that she could lever him away and free her hand, trapped between their sticky lower bellies.

Duncan rolled easily onto one hip, leaving a hairy leg slanting heavily across her sprawled knees, pinning them apart. He nuzzled into the soft side of her breast, inhaling deeply, flicking his tongue into the damp furrow where the swelling underslope met her delicate ribcage and, impossibly, she felt his sated manhood stir against her flank as he whispered, 'I'm sorry. You drove me so wild I forgot my manners, didn't I, darling? It should always be ladies first. Will you let me redeem myself?'

He took her slippery hand and pressed it down between her thighs and did something with it that had her hurtling off the edge of the planet, annihilating all her preconceived ideas about sexual fulfilment.

Oh, God, over a year later it still made her hot all over to remember what he had manipulated her into doing…and the way that he had watched—as if she had been doing it for *his* pleasure rather than hers alone…

'Kalera?'

Her eyes flew open, her body stiffening as she realised that she was in the middle of a public dance-floor. She blinked, dazed, at the man who had spoken her name, evidently—from the annoyance in his golden-brown eyes—not for the first time.

'Stephen?'

He was standing behind Duncan's shoulder, looking at her with a suspicious frown that made her wonder whether the scalding heat of her internal blush had turned her face scarlet, betraying her secret shame for all to see.

How long had she been wrapped up in her guilty memories? Far too long, judging from the fact that her fiancé had been impelled to come and fetch her. She suddenly became aware that rather than swirling around the dance-floor in socially acceptable fashion she and Duncan had been barely swaying in place, their bodies separated by a mere sliver of distance, his chin resting on the top of her head. Appalled by her abstraction, Kalera stepped hurriedly back, a skein of blonde silk unravelling between them as a few stray strands of her hair caught against the black velvet of his jacket, but instead of letting his arm drop from her waist Duncan moved with her, forcing Stephen to trail in their wake.

'Looks like the lady doesn't want you to cut in, Steve,' taunted Duncan, directing a malicious grin over his shoulder. 'Ouch!' He came to a stumbling halt as Kalera ground down on the toe of his boot with her delicate high heel.

'Sorry, did I hurt you?' she said, her narrow oval face smooth with innocence.

'Bruised me to the bone,' he said, with a little-boy-lost plaintiveness that didn't fool her for a moment.

'You'd better rush home and put some ice on it, then,' she suggested sweetly. 'Or you might end up with a limp.'

'Believe me, after dancing with you limpness is the least of my problems,' he retaliated *sotto voce*, his downy black lashes flickering as he glanced down his body.

'Kalera!' Stephen's clipped annoyance reminded her that once again she had allowed Duncan to distract her from the proper focus of her attention. 'I didn't come out here to dance. The chef is waiting to flambé your Triberg apples…you did say you wanted to see them cooked at the table.'

'Of course I do,' she said, turning sharply to break out of Duncan's grasp, carefully avoiding his eyes as she lifted her chin and said primly, 'Thank you for the dance.'

The jet earring on which she had fixed her gaze seemed to wink mockingly at her schoolgirl politeness. 'Oh, it was my pleasure, Kalera,' he said, allowing his fingers to trail down the length of her arm as she pulled it away. 'My very…*great*…pleasure.' The slow separation and languid emphasis of his words made them replete with innuendo. 'I know you enjoyed our *dancing* together as much as I did. You're a wonderfully…*gratifying*…dance partner. I envy the man who gets to…*dance* with you…on a regular basis.'

Kalera's ears burned. They both knew he wasn't talking about the two-step! 'Then you must envy Stephen,' she said deliberately, tucking her arm through her fiancé's elbow, aligning them together.

'Must I?' His brows sprang up and the charismatic grin flashed at full wattage. Too late she remembered that he knew she and Stephen weren't yet lovers. For an awful moment she thought he was going to reveal his knowledge with another sly innuendo.

'Yes!'

He dipped his head, acknowledging her desperation, his eyes brimming with mischief. 'Far be it from me to contradict a lady.'

'Since when have you cared about social niceties?' sniped Stephen. 'As I recall you've always preferred your women to be strictly of the tramp variety.'

Duncan's jaw tightened but he replied evenly, 'I suppose that depends on your interpretation of a woman— and a tramp. Personally, I thought the narrow-minded categorising of unattached females as either virgins or sluts had ended with the sexual revolution.'

'How very politically correct—but a rather specious argument considering your predilection for women who *are* attached,' said Stephen, covering Kalera's hand on his forearm with such possessive firmness that her shiny new ring dug into her fingers. 'For a fanatic about loyalty you have a fine disrespect for other people's vows of fidelity. Wife or fiancée—it makes no difference to you, does it? You simply take it as a challenge if a woman belongs to someone else.'

'And you think Kalera belongs to you?' Duncan's incredulity was a sneer in itself.

Stephen flashed his beautiful teeth in a tauntingly confident smile. 'I know she does!'

Kalera had a strong desire to bang their arrogant male heads together.

'Actually, I believe I belong to myself,' she stated tartly. Even when she was married to Harry she had kept a fair measure of her independence. 'A relationship is about partnership, not ownership!'

The two men looked at her with surprise, as if her opinion were an irrelevant intrusion, confirming her suspicion that their confrontation had little to do with her overstay on the dance-floor. It wasn't really about her at all; she was merely an excuse for them to score off each other. She scowled.

'I was referring to our *emotional* sense of belonging,' Stephen hastily assured her, dipping his golden head to bathe her in apologetic attention.

Kalera was mollified, but the lick of scorn in Duncan's navy eyes at her ready acceptance of Stephen's reassurance made her inwardly bristle. How dared he try to imbue her with doubts about her fiancé's sincerity?

She hugged Stephen's arm and smiled up at him with a brilliance that relaxed some of his underlying tension.

'I'm glad you came to find me—dancing has made

me quite peckish again. I hope this dessert is as mouth-watering as you promised it would be...' Repressed annoyance made her normally husky voice even throatier than usual, imparting a sexy resonance to the innocent statement. She began to turn and then paused, to deliver as a casual afterthought, 'Oh—goodnight, Duncan.'

He ran a hand through his inky-black hair, drawing it back from his temples to expose the prominent widow's peak that gave him a faintly devilish air as he challenged her unsubtle brush-off. 'Does this mean you're not going to offer me a bite of your apple?' He planted his hands on his hips, the flare of his short jacket exposing his perfect proportioning to her unwilling admiration. 'You know I wouldn't refuse—I can resist everything except temptation.'

His grin pronounced him every inch the unrepentant sinner.

'Precisely why I don't intend to place any in your way,' she replied acerbically. If he was referring to the fruit of knowledge, she thought that he had already dined spectacularly well enough off *that* particular tree!

When Duncan opened his mouth to respond, Stephen cut him off with a sternly punctuated dismissal.

'Good*night*, Royal!'

His nemesis threw up his hands in a mocking gesture of surrender but Duncan still managed to have the last, provocative word. 'Don't stay out too late, Kalera—remember you and I have a date for breakfast...'

'We have an early morning meeting with some clients at their hotel,' Kalera explained hastily, matching her shorter stride to Stephen's as he practically marched them off the floor. She didn't dare glance back for fear that Duncan might take it as an invitation, half expecting him to tag along anyway, for the sheer pleasure of stirring up more trouble. But for once he seemed capable of discreetly fading into the background.

The ghost of his unsettling presence, however, continued to hover in her consciousness, a spectre at the feast. At least with the chafing-dish already set up at the table any awkward questions from Stephen were postponed and Kalera glued her eyes with apparent fascination on the chef's hands as he swirled slices of peeled apple in a meld of butter, sugar, lemon juice and honey over the burner on his trolley. Unfortunately the price of her outer serenity was a churning stomach which cringed when the Kirsch was added and set alight.

The flames dancing across the sizzling fruit were unpleasantly evocative for one preoccupied with thoughts of temptation and sin. Surely sins of omission were at the lesser end of the scale? She was hardly likely to be condemned to an eternal roasting for not wanting to talk about a brief sexual encounter in her past. It wasn't as if she had ever actively *lied* about it...

'Thank you, this looks delicious.' She pinned on an enthusiastic smile to mask her sudden lack of appetite as the apples were spooned, still flaming, onto her plate and topped with a swirl of Kirsch-flavoured cream, adding richness to the heady, alcoholic aroma of caramelised apple.

Guiltily aware of Stephen's expectant gaze, Kalera forced herself to eat with every evidence of enjoyment and after the first few mouthfuls his attention thankfully shifted to his own portion, allowing her to ease back and toy with her dessert fork, dividing the apple into eversmaller pieces which she nudged under the leafy garnish at the edge of her plate.

She was furious with Duncan, and with herself for letting him get under her skin. She wanted no part of whatever game he was playing. His interference in her private life was unconscionable, unwelcome and unacceptable—and she intended to tell him so!

Her brooding glance flitted across the room as she mentally composed the cool reprimand she would deliver the next morning and her eyes widened at a glitter of gold-on-black. Duncan! Not only was he still in the restaurant, he was dining heartily at a distant table for two in the company of a tall, elegant brunette with bobbed hair and hands that darted expressively as she talked. Her fire-engine-red dress and blazing jewellery proclaimed a striking sense of style and her strongly etched profile indicated an aggressive self-confidence.

Just the sort of woman who would appeal to Duncan's flamboyant tastes, Kalera judged wryly—and not the type to take kindly to her handsome escort flitting off to dance with someone else, even if it *was* only his secretary. From the look of it Duncan was having to do some fast talking between bites. It would serve him right if his trouble-stirring had rebounded on himself. Kalera's gentle mouth tilted into a small, vengeful smile. She hoped the brunette was giving him a really hard time.

'Someone we know?' Stephen quizzed the direction of her gaze.

'I guess Duncan being here was a coincidence after all—he's evidently out on a dinner date himself,' she murmured, nodding towards the engrossed pair.

Stephen's fork clattered against his plate and Kalera saw him pale, then flush with renewed outrage.

'Bastard!' he muttered. Stephen—whose fastidious nature frowned on public cursing, who had retained his self-control even when Duncan had goaded him to his face!

'Do you know who she is?' she asked curiously.

'Yes, I know who she is,' Stephen echoed with a contemptuous snap, picking up his fork again and viciously skewering a piece of apple. 'Duncan was almost engaged to her once, but she decided to marry someone else. It didn't stop the two of them having a flaming affair, though, and by the look of it they're still going hot and strong…all lies to the contrary!'

His acrid bitterness gave Kalera a sinking feeling as she remembered the cryptic exchange of insults about ladies and tramps. She pursued the answer that she no longer wanted to hear. 'But who is she?'

Stephen's eyes were faintly sullen as they met her wary gaze. 'I think you've guessed already, haven't you? That, my dear, is Terri, my cheating ex-wife...and Duncan is the man that she was sleeping with for most of our marriage!'

CHAPTER FIVE

THE next morning Kalera went to work with a headache that no aspirin could cure.

Needless to say they hadn't lingered over liqueurs and on the uncomfortable journey home Kalera had learned more than she wanted to know about the extended death-throes of Stephen's seven-year marriage. She had listened to his bitter tale with a sinking heart, hearing the death-knell to any hopes she might have had of casually confessing her one-night stand with Duncan. Stephen would be incapable of viewing it objectively. Any other man he could have dismissed as no threat, but not Duncan. He would take Duncan as a personal insult, a twist of the knife that had already severed a large chunk of his masculine pride. How could he be expected to live comfortably with the knowledge that his hated rival had slept with *both* his wives?

In the darkness of the car Kalera's responses had been stilted, but fortunately Stephen had been too wrapped up in his own festering anger to notice her discomfiture.

He had admitted that relations with his wife had been rocky for some time leading up to the final, violent row, but he had hoped that his burgeoning suspicions about her mood swings, growing physical coldness and evasive behaviour would prove unfounded. To ease his mind he had hired a private detective and when he'd found out that his trust had been misplaced his bitterness had been intensified by the fact that, even when confronted with the detective's evidence of her persistent unfaithfulness, Terri had defiantly refused to explain or express any remorse over her actions. To his fury she had blamed *him* for wrecking the marriage with his mistrust, and had vowed that she was not going to allow him to also wreck her relationship with Duncan.

Stephen had said that he could have understood, if not forgiven, Terri's falling in love with someone else, but the cruel fact was that her affair with Duncan had been going on not just for weeks or for months, but for *years*—dating back to the time that they were in business together...

Although he'd railed fiercely against Terri for her treachery, Kalera had noticed that it was Duncan who was targeted with the worst of the blame.

'He hates my guts because I exposed him for what he is—a moral bankrupt. There's a dark, twisted side of him, the flip side to his brilliance, that's totally without conscience. He never wanted to marry Terri himself— he just couldn't stand the fact that I took her away from him and pulled the plug on our partnership, so he had to corrupt her, seduce her into playing his sick games, knowing that sooner or later I'd find out. Do you know what he did when I finally confronted him with the truth? He *laughed*!' Stephen spat out the word with choked loathing. 'He thought he'd won—that he'd proved his superiority over me yet again.

'But he was laughing on the other side of his face when I told him that I wasn't going to play the complacent husband.' The flash of a passing streetlight illuminated a smile of grim remembered satisfaction. 'That's what the two of them had counted on, you see—that I'd rather preserve the fiction of a happy family than hold myself up to public ridicule and contempt as the gullible poor sod who'd been cuckolded by his former best friend. They misjudged me then—as they do now. Why should I be upset that he flaunts Terri as his mistress? She's probably no more faithful to him than he is to her—they deserve each other as far as I'm concerned!'

But he *was* upset, if not by the sight of his ex-wife

with Duncan, then certainly by the necessity of raking over the painful memories for Kalera's sake. There was a white-hot edge to his anger which made her uneasy, but perhaps it was the continuing friction with Terri over the custody of young Michael that was constantly re-igniting his burning sense of injustice.

Kalera's own devastating experience of loss enabled her to understand why Stephen had kept his personal connection with Duncan secret. The greater the pain, the deeper one tried to bury it. What an awful irony it must have seemed when the one woman who had interested him since his divorce turned out to be working for his nemesis. No wonder he had seemed so appealingly vulnerable and cautious on those first few dates. He must have hesitated to commit himself to further involvement until he was sure that her relationship with Duncan was purely businesslike, the power of his attraction ultimately proving stronger than his fear of history repeating itself.

'I'm sorry. I should have told you all this before,' he said remorsefully as they kissed goodnight on her threshold. The leafy jasmine vine which grew over the porch trellis whispered above their heads, spilling its delicate fragrance into the warm night breeze. 'It wasn't very fair of me to keep you in the dark and still expect you to make an informed choice. I suppose you feel this puts you in an even more impossible position at work…?'

Kalera's first impulse was to agree, but her innate stubbornness made her baulk at the hint of manipulation. Stephen was a strong man with very firm opinions and she sometimes got the impression he would like to do the thinking for both of them.

'Awkward, perhaps, but not impossible,' she replied, feeling a throb of stress at her temples when his lips tightened. 'Maybe this is a good way of showing that we're not going to let the past taint our future. It's only for a few weeks. I'm not afraid of Duncan and you needn't be either. He has no power over our feelings for each other—'

'I'm not afraid, it's just—' He frowned down at her in the feeble glow of the jasmine-smothered porch light. 'I don't trust him...'

She almost smiled at the growled understatement. 'But you *do* trust me?'

His hesitation was barely noticeable. 'Of course I do.'

Her impulse to smile vanished. 'I'm *not* Terri,' she told him quietly. 'I would never, ever be unfaithful to my husband.'

'I know.' He knew he had hurt her and tried to gloss over his error. 'So...is this some kind of test of my faith?' he asked wryly.

She had instantly denied it, but this morning as she drove to the hotel where the breakfast meeting was being held she couldn't help wondering whether there wasn't a tiny element of truth in his joking remark. She could never marry where there was a lack of mutual trust. She pushed the fleeting doubt away. Nothing that she had learned in the last few hours challenged her fundamental understanding of Stephen as a sensitive, caring man who held steadfast to his ideals. It was her perspective of Duncan which had suddenly acquired a new and puzzling slant.

Stephen had made it sound almost as if Duncan had cold-bloodedly set out to seduce Terri from sheer masculine competitiveness but, while he thrived on challenge, Duncan was the least cold-blooded man that Kalera had ever met. The true source of his genius lay in the fierce passion with which he ignited his ideas in the minds of others. No goal was ever pursued half-heartedly, but always with reckless amounts of unbridled enthusiasm...whether it was creating a new piece of software or making love to a woman.

Kalera shivered as she pulled into the hotel car park, her nerves spiking at the vivid mental image of Duncan, his moon-burnished torso arched into a shuddering bow, his fists digging into the mattress, head flung back, sweat glistening on his straining throat, his mouth open on a hoarse cry of violent ecstasy as he spilled himself into her hand. Heat prickled over her breasts as she remembered how quickly his body had veered out of his control, his intellect completely submerged in a rapturous celebration of the senses.

She braked just before she hit the car-park wall, only her seat belt saving her from slamming her head against the steering wheel, and turned the ignition off with trembling fingers. No, a cold-blooded vendetta wasn't Duncan's style but she would well believe he might take any number of risks in the grip of hot-blooded passion!

To do what he had done he must have been deeply in love—it was the only motive that jelled with his character. Whether he had been in love with Terri before her marriage to Stephen, or not realised the overwhelming force of his emotions until later, the only thing that could have precipitated him into such a tortured affair would have been the discovery that his feelings were reciprocated. Add an innocent child to the volatile equation and the situation would have been even more fraught. Living a double life seemed so alien to Duncan's extroverted nature that it must have been Terri who had insisted on secrecy. Perhaps she had felt unable to choose between hurting her family and giving up the man she loved, until in the end the choice was made for her...

But if that was the case, why hadn't Duncan and Terri married each other as soon as she was free? Stephen spoke as though the affair was common knowledge but if so it wasn't considered sufficiently interesting to post on Labyrinth's bulletin board along with all the other gossip about Duncan's conquests...

Kalera was so distracted by her rampant speculations that she walked straight past Duncan in the hotel lobby and when he followed to tap her on the shoulder she almost leapt out of her skin.

'Nervous?' he asked smoothly as she spun on her trembling legs.

'Of what?' To her disgust her instant defensiveness made him chuckle. No wonder she hadn't noticed him; he was wearing camouflage—a dark grey pin-striped three-piece suit with a pale shirt and subdued tie that made her feel almost frivolous in her navy and white spotted spring dress.

She held her practical navy clutch bag to her fluttering stomach. 'All I have to do is take notes—nothing I haven't done hundreds of times before!'

'If not thousands,' he agreed blandly, shifting his laptop to his other hand and turning her in the direction of the restaurant. Her eyes flickered as she registered the pearl stud in his left ear, a twin to the discreet tie-pin that adorned his chest. Trust Duncan to find a way to express his individuality even in the midst of choking conformity.

He caught her peeking, his gaze lowering to her own earlobe. 'We make a good match, don't we? We were obviously attuned when we got dressed this morning.'

She immediately wanted to snatch the pearls that Harry had given her for their third anniversary out of her ears. 'It's hardly a matter of being attuned, since you must know I wear these to work most days of the week—'

'Must I? Do you think that the average boss notices every tiny feature of his secretary's appearance, every single day?' When she flushed he commented slyly, 'But you evidently think that *I* do. Does that mean that *you* notice everything about *me*?'

'You're not an *average* boss,' she rapped back, unconsciously increasing her pace as she evaded his question.

He stopped at the restaurant door, barring her way.

'Thank you; I'm glad you're willing to admit that we have a special relationship—'

'I *mean*…you're unusually observant and have a photographic memory for visual details.' She cut him off hastily, and then realised that it was not something that she wanted to dwell on—the fact that he could probably summon up a crease-by-freckle mental picture of her naked body!

'True, and this morning I observe there are little blue shadows under your eyes.' He dipped his head, a strand of blue-black hair falling across his brow as he lifted her chin with one finger to examine her more closely.

'Rough night?' His tone was sympathetic but his eyes were uncomfortably sharp.

'Not at all. I slept like a baby,' she lied haughtily.

'I didn't mean in bed,' he said, to her intense mortification. 'Steve gave me a filthy look as you guys left last night. He looked to be in a pretty mean temper…'

'I hope you're not suggesting he'd be physically abusive.' She jerked her face away from his disturbing touch, her grey eyes frosting over. 'Stephen is a gentleman; I know he'd never hurt me! Of course he was angry—what did you expect after the way you carried on? And then for him to see you were there with his *wife*—'

'His *ex*-wife.'

'That's what I said—'

'No, you said his *wife*. As if they were still irrevocably attached.'

'Yes, well, I *meant* his ex-wife.' She was flustered by her slip of the tongue, determined not to allow him to invest her mistake with any deep Freudian meanings. 'Anyway, she was still his wife when you, when you—' Her tongue got tangled up in her reluctance to continue and she moved aside as a group of businessmen brushed past them to push through the glass doors.

God, how had she wandered into this dangerous debate? It wasn't supposed to happen like this. She had told herself when she knocked back her aspirins in front of the bathroom mirror that she would greet him with a quiet ultimatum that he was to stop meddling in her private life or she would walk.

Now here she was delving into *his* private life!

'When I? What?' He had no right to sound so curious. He knew very well *what*!

She composed herself and fixed him with a firm stare, her husky voice taut with determination. 'It doesn't matter. Look, Duncan, perhaps now isn't the time to tell you this—'

The set of his shoulders tensed beneath the designer suit, his attention abruptly sliding past her to the interior of the restaurant and back again as he interrupted curtly, 'You're right, this isn't the time—our new clients are waiting—but I want you to know that I was way out of line last night. I should never have embarrassed you like that...'

She was sure she had misheard. 'I beg your pardon?'

'I'm sorry,' he said simply. He spread his hands, palm up, the grave penitent. 'If you hadn't turned up this morning it would have served me right. I behaved like an arrogant thug and you have every right to be mad. It was wretched of me, unforgivable...well, not quite, I hope. But I put you in a horrible spot and that was wrong of me.' He shook his head. 'Harry would have been disgusted at my performance—he always claimed I was too much of a drama queen—he said that's why I could never beat him on the golf course...I threw too many of my clubs into the lake!'

As always, the mention of Harry made her feel soft inside and she had practically turned to mush by the time Duncan had finished grovelling his remorse. His cheerful self-abasement cut the ground neatly from under Kalera's feet, so that she found herself accepting his apology feeling as if *she* might have been the one who had overreacted!

'You should have been a lawyer,' she grumbled as he pushed open the door to the restaurant with far too white a grin for a man who had just covered himself with sackcloth and ashes.

'Like dear old Dad? No, thanks; too many boring precedents to follow. I tried law, you know, after I dropped out of Med School, but it definitely wasn't my scene.' His smile mocked his own youthful fickleness. 'Nothing really clicked for me until I took time off from university to work for Terri's father's America's Cup yachting syndicate and discovered computers. Up to that point my parents were convinced I was going to end up as an over-educated bum.'

She hadn't known, but it didn't surprise her to learn that he hadn't followed a straight and narrow academic path like his father, an eminent QC. Since Duncan now possessed a doctorate along with his fame and fortune, the hell-raising at high school and undergraduate level to which Stephen had disparagingly referred had obviously been the restlessness of a brilliant mind as yet unfocussed.

The deal discussed over smoked salmon and scrambled eggs secured Duncan a small corporate contract for a security and access management program which Labyrinth was launching the following month. But Duncan had shrewdly picked the small corporation as being at the leading edge of a growth industry, and was confident that getting in on the ground floor would ensure big future profits for its network software developer.

Watching him translate his dazzling techno-vision of the future into language the CEO could understand without condescending to the man's fresh-faced, gee-whiz-kid information systems manager reminded Kalera all over again of how much she loved her job and what a wrench it would be to leave all this vicarious excitement behind.

Later, watching Duncan high-five around the office

sharing the good news, she felt for the first time immune from the infectious air of celebration, realising that she wouldn't be around to see the contract honoured. In fact, she wasn't quite certain *where* she'd be in a month's time, and the thought sent a brief flutter of panic jumping along her nerves. She had moved too many times in her childhood, lived among too many strangers, to view the prospect of radical change with anything but apprehension, and the sudden, traumatic loss of her husband had merely reinforced her fear of emotional displacement.

But she had Stephen now, she consoled herself. He, too, was seeking emotional security, and their needs seemed to dovetail so perfectly that it was natural that their mutual desire for companionship had so swiftly turned to romance. But they were both too cautious to allow themselves to be swept away by its momentum. Getting engaged had been a big step—just how big Kalera hadn't realised until she had stumbled up against Duncan's furious opposition!

And Duncan wasn't the only one. The news of her controversial engagement spread through the Labyrinth network like wildfire and over the next few days Kalera found herself inundated with friendly advice. A few people, mostly women, offered their congratulations unencumbered, but the rest of the responses ranged from mild dismay to rowdy disapproval.

'I suppose he *is* pretty spunky-looking,' conceded Anna Ihaka as they were both touching up their make-up in the women's restroom. Kalera followed her gaze to the picture of Stephen, scanned from the *Financial Star* by some anonymous joker and reprinted with the famous red circle-and-slash 'No' graphic adorning his smiling face, which was tacked to the wall beside the mirror. The posters had begun appearing all over the office after Duncan had confirmed her impending defection, and Kalera had given up trying to track down the mysterious perpetrator. Whenever she took one down, two popped up in its place.

'Thanks,' she said, powdering the sheen off her nose. 'But I'm not marrying him for his looks…'

'Sure—but no one wants to fall for a complete gargoyle, right?' said Anna, who fell in and out of love with monotonous regularity and consequently considered herself something of an expert on romance. 'I mean, let's face it, a guy with a gorgeous bod has a natural advantage over a homely little creep with personality. Who would you rather be seen out with? And when your eyes go zing with a stranger across a crowded room it's because you're thinking, Wow, that guy looks *hot*! Not, Gee, what an attractive personality!' She whisked some blusher over her cheekbones and started applying another layer of brilliant gloss to her lips.

'Yes, well, fortunately Stephen has both,' said Kalera, snapping her compact closed and taking out her lipstick. She had to admit that there had been an element of vanity in her acceptance of that first date—she had been flattered that such an elegant, urbane man was interested in her rather ordinary company.

Anna blotted her lips with a paper towel. 'Someone said you met at a wild party?'

No doubt that 'someone' had relayed the facts with his usual flair for subjective embellishment. Duncan had employed Anna five years ago straight from school on the strength of a few meetings on the Internet, and despite her cheeky irreverence she was still inclined to accept his every word as gospel.

'It was a very sedate sit-down dinner. We got talking and liked each other so we ended up talking some more—'

'Doesn't sound very exciting,' Anna said dubiously.

Kalera outlined the bow of her upper lip. 'Neither of us was looking for excitement,' she said, blocking in the rest of the colour. 'But I guess it found us anyway,' she added wryly, thinking of the furore their engagement had created.

Anna shovelled her make-up back into her shiny black bag. 'Yeah, well…I think it's too weird,' she sighed. 'I mean, I always thought that, if you got it on with *any-one*, for sure it would be the chief.'

Kalera's lipstick clattered into the ceramic basin and she scrabbled to pick it up, screening the panic in her eyes with her lowered lashes. 'Why on earth would you think that?' she croaked.

Anna shrugged, her cropped top revealing a flash of brown skin above her wildly patterned leggings as she leaned forward to check the disposition of her beaded locks. ''Cos he's been crazy about you for years, I suppose.'

'Don't be ridiculous,' muttered Kalera, stunned into stammering confusion. 'He—I—he—Harry…'

Amazingly Anna seemed to understand her incoherent fumblings. 'Oh, I know he was happy to, you know, like— worship you from afar with his respect and all that while he thought you were still hung up about losing Harry, but jeez, you must have noticed he behaves differently around you… He doesn't flirt the way he does with other women, and he's always sort of gentle—you know, as if he's trying to slow himself down to your speed…'

'No, I don't know!' choked Kalera. As far as she was concerned Duncan had only one speed and that was a hundred kilometres per hour! 'For goodness' sake, Anna, it's too absurd for words.' She went hot and cold with alarm. 'Oh, God, don't tell me everyone else thinks that too?'

Anna sniffed. 'Of course not! As Duncan's assistant I'm around you two a lot more than most people and guess I pick up on the little things that nobody else notices—'

'Good, because the idea is totally off the wall,' Kalera

interrupted. 'Duncan and I are absolute polar opposites; we have practically *nothing* in common…'

But Anna's fertile romantic imagination was immune to logic. 'Right—and everyone knows that opposites attract!'

Kalera reeled from the restroom, shell-shocked, and ran slap-bang into Duncan striding down the hall.

He gripped her by the arms as she rebounded off his chest, his eyebrows rising at the sight of her unusually flushed face.

'What's up? Not coming down with summer flu, are you?' He let go of one of her arms and applied his cool knuckles to her hot cheek.

'I'm fine,' fibbed Kalera, shying away from the casual intimacy of his touch, acutely conscious that at any moment Anna was going to come bouncing through the door behind her, and would no doubt see the little tableau as proof of her wild speculations.

Duncan's gaze moved thoughtfully to the closed door and back to Kalera's deepening blush.

'Are they still giving you a hard time?' he murmured. 'Would you like me to pass the word around to lay off?'

In her hypersensitive state Kalera detected the hint of smugness in his proffered sympathy. Duncan was pleased by his staff's partisan display.

Her chin rose. 'I can handle it. After all, it's only for a few more weeks,' she pointed out, shrugging off his concern along with his staying hand.

Just in time. As Duncan's eyes darkened in annoyance at the tart reminder Anna barrelled out into the hallway and stopped dead, looking hopefully from one to the other.

'Sorry, am I interrupting something?'

'Definitely not!' said Kalera, with what she instantly realised was a shade too much emphasis.

Duncan immediately scooped up the initiative. 'In the

hall?' He returned his assistant's mischievous grin. 'You've got to be kidding! You know me—I'm the soul of discretion.'

'It's facetious comments like *that* that fuel the stupid rumours,' Kalera chastised him severely as he followed her into her office. 'Everyone knows what a flagrant exhibitionist you are!'

'Being uninhibited isn't the same as being loose-tongued,' he murmured, 'but it certainly provides protective camouflage. I built my business on being able to guard my secrets, remember? I can be as close as the grave when it really matters.' He bent down and planted his palms on her desk as she pretended to busy herself with a shuffling of paper. 'Is there one stupid rumour in particular that's upset you?'

Heat swarmed over her body and the teasing glint of amusement in Duncan's eyes sharpened into curiosity as Kalera mumbled something evasive. She wasn't going to embarrass herself further by repeating Anna's absurd opinions out loud.

'You do know you can talk to me about anything, Kalera,' he said, lowering his voice persuasively. 'I'm very open-minded and pretty well unembarrassable.'

She flashed him an exceedingly dry look.

It was her own precious peace of mind she was concerned about, not his. Even the mere *thought* of telling him that he was supposedly crazy about her sent hot shivers skittering along her nerves.

Any woman who was loved by Duncan Royal was headed for a life of constant turmoil!

Unfortunately, instead of sinking into the deep, dark recesses of memory the mad idea persisted in hanging around on the fringes of her consciousness, a burden of dangerous knowledge that made her feel unfairly guilty, and which fired her determination to preserve a prudent professional distance between herself and Duncan.

* * *

If only he had been equally committed to her graceful withdrawal from Labyrinth Technology it might have worked, but Duncan was proving annoyingly uncooperative. A case in point was the employment of her replacement, which should have been a straightforward matter of picking the best person for the job.

'Duncan, she can't even *spell*!' Kalera cried in exasperation as they discussed the latest candidate on the third morning of interviews.

'That's why word-processing programs have spell-checking utilities,' he replied airily.

'Look here—she even got the word Labyrinth wrong...*twice!*'

Duncan didn't even glance down at the document that Kalera had shoved across his desk. He shrugged, rocking his black leather swivel chair back and forth. 'Nerves. She was probably put off by you sitting there glowering at her while she was trying to concentrate.'

Kalera's smooth brow ruffled with distaste. 'I was *not* glowering.'

'Well, you weren't very friendly.'

She set her teeth. 'It was a job interview, not an invitation to join a social club!'

'Yes, well...you know how I feel about formality. *I* thought Lara was fun.'

Kalera controlled a sudden desire to scream. He was being deliberately obtuse. In the last few days he had become infuriatingly slippery when she'd tried to pin him down to making a serious decision.

'We're not looking for "fun", we're looking for competent,' she articulated crisply.

Duncan linked his hands behind his head and kicked back in his chair, swinging his feet up onto his desk.

Kalera eyed the scuffed running shoes with trailing laces nudging the edge of his keyboard. Only Duncan could come to work in an Armani suit one day and turn up in chain-store jeans and plain white T-shirt the next, although the eye-catching stainless-steel Alain Silberstein watch on his wrist had probably cost him the equivalent of two designer suits. He rolled his head against his hands and the stud in his left ear snagged at her temper. Why did he always have to be so aggressively *different*? Being unique was almost some sort of fetish with him. Why, even in bed he—

Her thoughts screeched to a halt. *No*, she was *not* going to think about it any more!

'We want to hire someone with practical skills, not simply an ability to make you laugh,' she ground out.

Duncan flexed his elbows behind his head, the bleached white cotton straining across his torso, revealing a dark shadow where the hair curled thickly on his chest. Kalera knew exactly how soft and luxuriant that growth was, how sensuously springy it felt against her bare skin. She licked her dry lips as he continued, 'Lara had other qualities.'

'Name two!' she foolishly challenged.

He pretended to consider and a wolfish smile prowled across his face. 'Her legs.'

The candidate had indeed worn a mini-skirt that was barely decent, but Kalera knew when she was being taken for a ride.

'She doesn't type with her legs,' she said coolly, sitting back in her chair. 'In fact, judging from this—' she flicked the dictation test '—she doesn't type at *all*! And since I know you'd never hire a woman simply for her looks—'

'I hired you, didn't I?'

She bristled. 'I *presumed* it was because I had the best qualifications.'

She had graduated top of her secretarial class, to the despair of her parents who had considered it a diploma in repression and a betrayal of her roots. 'But you can't be truly creative in an *office*,' her mother had cried when she had told them she was taking the course. 'It's so sterile and unimaginative. You'll end up as a slave to routine, a prisoner to technology!'

To Kalera, her parents' fanatical adherence to the teachings of the latest feel-good guru was a more constrictive form of slavery, but of course they didn't see it that way.

Duncan shook his head, his eyes heavy-lidded with amusement.

'True, but that's not the primary reason I chose you. I knew as soon as I saw you walk through that door that I wanted you...' he paused a dangerous beat '...for my secretary. I assure you, I was acting on pure instinct—I hadn't even read your CV.'

'And now your instinct's telling you that a grammatically challenged bottle-blonde with legs up to her ears and a single-figure IQ is my perfect replacement!'

Kalera bit her lip as her bitchiness echoed in her ears, for all the world as if she were a jealous wife. But her objections were purely logical, she told herself fiercely. Lara might well be a very nice girl—but Duncan needed someone mature in charge of his office, someone coolheaded who could keep her feet on the ground when he was bouncing off the walls. The last thing he needed was another breathless admirer pandering to his reckless genius.

'Actually, my idea of a perfect replacement for you is *you*,' he replied smoothly. 'So...how about it?'

She ignored the blatant provocation. 'If we don't find a replacement by the time I'm due to leave—don't expect me to extend my notice,' she warned, voicing the lurking suspicion that he might be spinning out the process to just that end.

'In that case we'd better stop wasting time and get back to work,' Duncan said, glittering a smile at her that showed no sign of guilt or remorse. 'I hope you haven't made any lunch plans because it looks like we'll have to work straight through...I'll send out for some sandwiches. And I'll probably have to ask you to stay on late again this evening, as well.'

Kalera opened her mouth to object, and then changed her mind. Stephen had been supposed to phone to let her know whether he was free to meet her for lunch, but since it was already mid-morning and he hadn't yet done so it was probably safe to assume he, too, would be busy during her lunch-hour. She could save her protests and her dignity, and offend no one by her compliance.

CHAPTER SIX

SHE discovered her mistake later that afternoon when she paused at the temporarily unoccupied reception desk to answer the unattended telephone, and found an irate Stephen on the other end of the line.

'I've been trying to get through to you all day but that damned receptionist keeps telling me you're unavailable.'

Kalera bit her lip. 'You should have left a message—'

'I did, several times, but you never replied to any of them—I assume they were never passed on.' Stephen's voice rose in outrage as he continued, 'And when I called by to pick you up for lunch Royal's bully-boy excuse for a security man refused to send word up to you that I was there.'

'Oh, dear,' said Kalera feebly. She had no doubt that the orders to censor Stephen's calls and messages had been issued by Royal decree.

Nor, apparently, had Stephen. 'It's just petty vindictiveness. You tell Duncan you're not going to tolerate his blatant interference in your private life.'

'Well, I suppose he *could* claim he's within his rights as an employer to place a restriction on personal phone calls during business hours...' said Kalera, striving to be fair. Before their engagement became public Stephen had never phoned her at work and she couldn't help thinking that it was a mite tactless of him to expect loyal Labyrinthians to instantly embrace the enemy.

Stephen's voice chilled several degrees. 'Are you *defending* him?'

'No, no, of course not,' she said hurriedly, seeing

Kirsty Seymour trotting back to the reception desk, a cup of coffee in hand. 'Look, I must go—I'm sorry about lunch, but I wouldn't have been able to leave the office anyway; we were just too busy—'

'Well, how about tonight? Mother's invited me over for dinner but I can ring her and say you're coming too...'

'I'm afraid I'll be working late tonight as well,' she said, her tone of regret disguising a guilty twinge of relief. She and Madeline Prior politely tolerated each other for Stephen's sake but Kalera had never felt truly comfortable in her prospective mother-in-law's company. She knew that Madeline had doted on Terri and still maintained close contact with her son's former wife by regularly baby-sitting little Michael. Kalera, with her unconventional upbringing and brazenly eccentric parents, was a dubious addition to Madeline's carefully cultivated social circle. Added to which was Kalera's uneasy suspicion that, although she had never said so out loud, the older woman secretly held her somehow responsible for Stephen's continuing estrangement from his son.

'What—*again*?'

'It won't be for very much longer,' she soothed, crossing her fingers. Duncan couldn't continue to keep her late *every* night, not without seriously disrupting his *own* social life. He would soon get bored with his game, especially if she persisted in acting unperturbed by his attempts to sabotage her evenings. 'Once I start training my replacement I'll make sure she takes on the overtime.'

'So, he has settled on one, then...'

'Actually, no, we're still at the interviewing stage,' Kalera confessed, and then nibbled anxiously at her lip, wondering whether even that innocent remark was revealing too much.

There was a small silence. 'I suppose he's still trying

to con you into changing your mind?' He didn't wait for an answer. 'Oh, well…at least that means there's still a chance for my mole to clinch the job.'

The sharp edge to Stephen's sardonic comment gave Kalera a moment's uncertainty before she laughed. Of *course* he was joking! Even if Stephen were to go to such absurd lengths to try and plant one of his employees at Labyrinth, he certainly wouldn't tip his hand by boasting about it on an open phone line.

Nevertheless, she couldn't help, as she rang off, harbouring a tiny niggle of doubt.

'Thanks for picking that up,' said Kirsty, setting down her coffee perilously close to her keyboard as she collapsed back in her swivel chair. 'I just nipped along the hall for a cup of stamina—I went to an ace party last night and I'm still feeling a bit ragged. Was it an important call?'

'It was as far as I was concerned…it was Stephen.'

'Oh!' Kirsty blushed with a redhead's easy brilliance, her fresh, freckled face drenched in guilt. 'I…er…'

Kalera took pity on her. 'Don't worry, I know you were only obeying orders from on high.' She turned back towards Duncan's office, tossing over her shoulder with a crispness that made Kirsty surreptitiously grin, 'Expect to shortly have them countermanded!'

Duncan, however, when confronted by his perfidy, stood staunchly by his view that it was a simple security matter—he didn't want his chief rival to have easy access to Labyrinth's communications system and thus the opportunity to hack into the network.

'Easy! I thought you said your new firewall was impenetrable without the proper encryption codes,' scoffed Kalera.

He swivelled his chair gently back and forth, looking up into her indignant face. 'As of this moment, yes. But let's face it, in Cyberspace there's always someone coming up with something newer than new. Someone with the will, the skill, the time and the resources might figure a way to crack the encryption or bypass the codes. And there's always the risk of human error opening up a window of opportunity.'

'If you don't trust me I don't see why you want me continuing in your employ,' Kalera said stiffly.

Duncan's voice dropped to a husky drawl, a counterpoint to the expensive creak of leather as he leaned forward in his chair to cover the hand she had planted on his desk. 'Darling, you know that I'd trust you to the ends of the earth with the cherished secrets of my soul...'

The outrageously flattering words were uttered with such fervent sincerity that Kalera's whole body was suffused by a traitorous warmth. Her breath clogged in her lungs as she became aware of the intimacy of the admiration in the navy eyes and the searing familiarity of his touch. For a brief instant she was transported back into a darkened bedroom where she had wantonly invited his admiration and recklessly sought pleasure from those clever, caressing fingers.

With a gasp she snatched her tingling hand from his warm grip and his mouth twisted into a wry smile as he added, 'It's *him* I don't trust.'

Implying that she shouldn't either!

Kalera sniffed to express her disdain and assumed a detached politeness for the rest of the afternoon which only faltered when she returned from doing some photocopying and ran into Bryan Eastman, head of their research division, coming out of Duncan's office, an unaccustomed grimness pulling his thin, pale face into tight lines of anxiety.

Bryan was as close to the typical preconception of a computer nerd as Duncan was distant. He was short and as skinny as a rail, myopic and, with his prematurely thinning sandy hair, wispy beard and hunched gait, always looked much older than his twenty-five years. He was utterly dedicated to his work, but his juvenile sense of humour and penchant for practical jokes rescued him from being a complete obsessive.

When he saw Kalera he pinned on a weak smile but his light blue eyes skated anxiously away from hers as they paused to exchange pleasantries. Instead of lingering as he usually did to ask after Anna, on whom he had a massive unrequited crush, he edged quickly out of the conversation, the deep frown returning to his bony brow as he hurried off down the hallway.

Duncan was on his feet staring out of the window when she re-entered his office and, studying the set of his back and his uncharacteristic stillness, she forgot that she was supposed to be punishing him with her aloofness.

'What's the matter with Bryan? Is there a problem with "Janet and John"?' she asked as she placed the copied reports he had requested on his desk. Since Bryan practically lived at Labyrinth and had no personal life to speak of she couldn't imagine anything but work could cast him into such gloom. Although she knew none of the technical details, she was aware that his research team was in the final stages of developing a piece of multi-language speech-recognition software under the codename of the old-fashioned children's reading primer.

Duncan turned slowly and looked at her with a strangely shuttered expression, almost as if he didn't see her, then he blinked and his moment of abstraction passed. He padded back towards his desk, a dangerous smile prowling across his firm mouth. As he got closer she could see that his navy eyes were alight with a fierce exhilaration, a classic sign that his imaginative intelligence was responding to a fresh challenge.

'Nothing I can't handle.'

Kalera waited for him to expand on the bald statement with his usual aggressive optimism, but instead he picked up the reports and silently flicked through the pile.

'Bryan looked really worried. Is it going to mean a delay to the project?' Kalera prodded, knowing that Duncan believed 'Janet and John' had the potential to become one of Labyrinth's international top-sellers, superseding all similar programs currently on the market. He had certainly made a huge investment of money and resources, and at this late stage of development time was of the essence.

His long, dark lashes continued to screen his gaze. 'Not necessarily.'

The casual, dismissive tone grated.

'Is that the equivalent of telling me not to worry my pretty little head about it?' Kalera said tartly.

His head tilted and he finally looked directly at her again, his eyebrows rising mockingly.

'Since you're not planning to be around for the project's completion there doesn't seem much point in involving you, does there?' he murmured. His smile smouldered provocatively around the edges as he watched her grey eyes grow sullen with chagrin at the undeniable truth of his statement. He thrust the reports at her. 'Here. File these, will you?'

Her chagrin turned to puzzlement. 'But you asked me to make you extra hard copies.'

'So?' he responded imperiously. 'Now I want the copies filed.'

Muttering under her breath, she complied, but as she tackled the redundant chore it occurred to her that Duncan had asked for the photocopying to be done just after he had received a brief phone call on his direct internal line, to which he had replied in unrevealing monosyllables.

Had Bryan been the caller? Had Kalera been discreetly got out of the way in anticipation of his visit?

She slammed the filing cabinet shut and leant against

it, her throat suddenly tight as she unconsciously twisted the elaborate engagement ring on her finger. She shouldn't really be surprised if she was being cut out of the information loop, but it was disturbing to realise how much it hurt to be excluded from Duncan's magic inner circle. Maybe she wasn't quite as ready for major changes in her life as she had thought?

A hollow opened up in her stomach as the reality of what she was doing fully crashed in on her. She wasn't simply grafting a new life onto the old one, as most people did when they moved on to a new relationship. With her marriage to Stephen she was completely severing the links that bound her to the world which she and Harry had inhabited. When she sold the house and moved into Stephen's home as his wife there would be no going back, no casual friendly contact with her former colleagues and friends; and especially not with Duncan...

A faint flutter of panic beat in her chest and she fought it down. For her own peace of mind she must keep herself firmly focussed on the future. Soon she and Stephen would be building new memories together that would overlie the potent images of the past, muting their power to disturb.

Unfortunately that serene future was still frustratingly far away. As yet she was still stuck in the present, prey to a barrage of conflicting feelings, some of which had no place in the mind of a newly engaged woman.

With relief Kalera found that the last two interviewees of the day were reassuringly competent secretaries who were more interested in working conditions and rates of pay than the masculine charms of their prospective employer. To her annoyance she couldn't quite banish the echo of Stephen's silly joke about a mole and was disgusted to find herself thinking that maybe their qualifications were *too* good. One was a grandmother and the other a *soignée* woman in her thirties who rather startlingly announced just before the termination of her interview that she was gay—'because I don't want it to become an issue later'.

'I don't see why it should,' said Duncan equably. 'I don't usually query my employees' sexual orientation. My only concern would be if it rendered them vulnerable to blackmail but your frankness obviously negates any security risk on that score.'

'She's the best so far,' commented Kalera as the woman left.

'Why do you say that? Because she's gay?'

Kalera recoiled under Duncan's challenging stare. 'No, of course not! Because of her qualifications—'

'Which are no better than some of the ones you've given a swift thumbs-down to. It seems to me that you've suddenly developed an intriguing prejudice against your own sex. Have you noticed that the only candidates you've wholeheartedly approved of so far are either male, over fifty, married with children or lesbian?'

'I—you—' Kalera floundered for a moment before she rallied. 'What about the Gatherfield woman?'

'Ugly as sin and sour as unripe lemons.' He propped his elbow on the desk and plopped his chin into his hand, a picture of smugness. 'Face it, Kalera, you don't want me to have a young and attractive and emotionally unattached woman flitting around as my secretary. And since I have an unblemished record as an employer it can't be the unsuspecting females you're protecting...so I guess it must be *me*...'

'Nonsense!' she sputtered, gathering up the interview notes with fumbling fingers, mangling the paper clip as she tried to jam too many sheets into its grip.

'Is it? You're sure you're not letting jealousy get in the way of your professional judgment?'

'Don't be silly,' she choked, her outrage undermined by the sneaking fear that there might be some substance in his allegation. She jumped to her feet, anxious to halt the dangerous drift of the conversation. 'I have no reason to be jealous—'

'No, you don't.' Duncan rose and shadowed her nervous movements on the other side of the desk. 'No matter how attractive or alluring she is, I'll never feel about another secretary the way I feel about you…thank God!'

The heartfelt addition made her hand clench involuntarily on the papers in her grasp and the end of the distorted paper clip speared sharply into her thumb, providing a welcome distraction from the threat of his words. 'Ouch!'

'What have you done? Let me see.' Duncan wove himself sinuously around the end of his desk and divested her of the weapon. He tossed the papers back down on his desk and turned her hand over and they both looked down at the bead of blood rapidly forming on the pad of her thumb.

'Here. Let me.' Expecting him to offer up his handkerchief to dab at the tiny wound, Kalera was stunned speechless when he lifted her hand and put her entire thumb in his mouth, his tongue swirling over the tip as he suckled strongly. She froze, her thoughts turning to chaos. His cheeks hollowed and as she stared into his deep, dark gaze the hot, wet, rhythmic contractions suddenly became shockingly erotic.

She tugged at her hand and felt his teeth clamp lightly around the base of her thumb, anchoring it in place. His fingers slid to her wrist, picking up her wildly fluctuating pulse as his rasping tongue shafted down the plump column of flesh in his mouth, sucking harder, drawing her more deeply into the sensual intimacy of the moment.

Kalera made an inarticulate sound which she later liked to think was a protest and pushed her other hand flat against his rock-hard chest, splaying over the harsh thump of his heartbeat and discovering that it was every bit as erratic as her own.

'Duncan, do you think—? *Woops!*' Anna did an

abrupt U-turn, the beads on her braids rattling with the swiftness of her spin as she scampered out again. 'I'll come back again when you're not so—uh—preoccupied…'

Kalera felt dizzy with dismay and something else she didn't dare examine.

'Now look what you've done! Stop that!' she hissed belatedly, stiffening knees that were showing an alarming tendency to sag. Her fingertips curled warningly into Duncan's cheek, her neat nails making a row of tiny indentations in the taut olive skin. 'Let me go…now!'

The smouldering gaze never left hers as Duncan slowly pulled her glistening thumb from his mouth and then pushed it tauntingly back in again, his teeth grazing lazily across her slick flesh, before finally withdrawing it to rest against his lips.

'I just wanted to make sure the blood flowed to clean the wound,' he murmured innocently, taking one last lick, his fingers still firm around her slender wrist. 'I don't want you getting an infection.'

'It was only the tiniest pin-prick, for goodness' sake,' she protested unevenly. 'You didn't have to go overboard. Oh, God, imagine what Anna must be thinking!'

She groaned, remembering their conversation in the restroom. Duncan's assistant needed no encouragement to let her imagination run riot.

'What does it matter what she thinks?'

Kalera glared at him, a far cry from the usual serene office Madonna. 'She might tell everyone what she saw!'

'It's not as if we were even kissing,' Duncan pointed out, although in Kalera's opinion a kiss could hardly have been more intimate. 'So you had your thumb in my mouth. What's so wicked about that? Be thankful it was only your thumb!' he added drolly.

She went scarlet, squirming in his grip, her voice shrill with outrage. '*Duncan!*'

He kissed her wrist and let it slip through his fingers. 'Well, it could have been your toes,' he mocked. 'That *would* have been difficult to explain away.' He correctly interpreted her stunned expression. 'No, Kalera, I don't have a secret foot fetish—I've never sucked a woman's toes in my life.' His eyelids drooped. 'But I'm always open to new experiences...'

'You don't understand,' she said, backing away, curling her damp thumb into her protective fist. 'You've got to set her straight. She already thinks that you—that you—' She faltered at his look of intense curiosity.

'That I what?' He hitched his hip on the corner of his desk and tilted his head to one side, his eyes bright on her rosy face.

She knew this was a mistake. 'You know...have a—a *thing*...' she mumbled.

The corners of his mouth crept up. 'A thing? I have a *thing*?'

'Yes,' she gritted, folding her arms across her waist.

'That's a noun that covers a whole lot of ground...a fair bit of it minefield. Can you be a bit more specific? What kind of a *thing* is it that I have, Kalera?'

'About me,' she said tightly.

'Oh!' He pantomimed dawning enlightenment. 'You mean *that* kind of *thing*! She thinks I have a mental preoccupation with you as the passionate object of my burning desire.'

'Something like that,' she muttered, hunching her shoulders to present a smaller target for his mockery. Busy avoiding his gaze, she didn't see his expression alter to one of brooding ruefulness.

'Clever Anna,' he said softly. 'And here I thought the carefree playboy routine had everybody fooled.'

Kalera's eyes flew to his face, her delicate body tensing for flight at the raw emotion that blazed in the dark eyes, sending a sizzle of familiar heat streaking along her veins. As if her fear had tripped an alarm the blaze was instantly extinguished and she could almost believe that she had imagined the shattering intensity of that look, and her shamefully ready response.

'Don't worry, I'll make sure that Anna understands,' he said, and she was so busy denying what had just happened that she failed to notice that he didn't pinpoint exactly what it was he was going to ensure Anna understood.

'Now, why don't we both compare notes on those we interviewed today and then we can start reviewing our strategies for tomorrow's list? And I want to get letters out tonight to all those who don't make today's cut— it's not fair to keep people dangling any longer than absolutely necessary when they might need to reply to other job offers. *Personal* letters, too, not form things that make the rejectee feel even less of an individual.'

He saw her glance at her watch, mentally calculating whether the tasks would fit into the time available.

'And I need you to print out some files for Bryan— preferably when there's no one else around,' he said, unfolding himself from his perch. 'I did warn you I might need you to stay on this evening.'

It took an effort not to step back as he towered over her, but the hint of satisfaction in his tone goaded her to dig her heels in.

'So you did,' she agreed, ironing her face into the serene indifference that she knew he found so infuriating.

'So…if you and Steve were going somewhere special tonight you'd better call him and cancel. Tell him you don't know what time you'll be finishing.' He swept an expansive hand towards his desk. 'You can use my phone if you like, and be sure to pass on my regrets for keeping his fiancée from his side…'

She widened her grey eyes. 'I thought I wasn't allowed to use your phone lines to talk to Stephen,' she said piously.

'Well, I can't let you just stand him up, can I? The poor guy deserves to know why his romantic evening has crashed and burned. Go ahead—I won't listen,' he offered magnanimously, when they both knew that his ears would be madly flapping to catch every single syllable.

'Actually we had no arrangements for tonight,' she said, dashing his hopes with gentle relish. 'Stephen is having a quiet dinner with his mother, at her place.'

'Oh, *Madeline...*' Duncan rolled his eyes in perfect understanding. 'The Queen Bee—or do I mean Bore? What's the matter, weren't you invited?'

She gave him a haughty look that failed to quell his curiosity, or his unfortunate powers of perception. He grinned. 'Ah-ha, so you *were* invited and you managed to wriggle out of it.' His eyes danced with mischief. 'I don't blame you; I never got on with Madeline, either. She thought I was a bad influence on her angelic little darling—a swarthy sinner beside his shining blond purity—hence I was always the one who took the blame for his wrongdoings. *Plus ça change* and all that, huh?'

'Madeline and I get on perfectly well,' countered Kalera, grateful that the truth was obligingly elastic.

'As long as you don't transgress her stuffy rules of polite conversation,' guessed Duncan, revealing a shrewd knowledge of his subject. 'Even then she'd probably grin and bear it—after all, you were chosen by her son, who can do no wrong. Has she shown you all her home videos, yet, of Stephen's boyish accomplishments and manly achievements? Ah, I see by your glazed expression that she has, and Madeline being Madeline she probably made you sit through the wedding one, as well, just so she could point out all her pedigreed friends.

'So how *did* you avoid the jaw-cracking prospect of a comfortable coze with Mumsie? Is that why old Steve was pestering you on the phone earlier?' he figured slyly. 'What did you do—trot out the hoary old line about working late at the office?' He hooted gleefully at her betraying wince.

'Since it happens to be the truth it's hardly a line,' Kalera said, clinging to her dignity.

'No wonder you didn't raise a whimper of protest about my slave-driving,' he grinned. 'It's saved you from a fate worse than death. Now you won't have to lie if Steve gets suspicious and checks up on your story.'

She drew in a sharp breath. 'He wouldn't do that. There's no reason for him to be suspicious!'

Duncan's shrug was one of wry cynicism. 'That's never stopped him before.'

He paused before saying with a quiet lack of emphasis, 'I bet whenever you say you're going out somewhere without him he always rings you at home later to see what time you're back home...'

'That's because he's such a gentleman,' she said, wondering why she should suddenly feel so defensive over Stephen's flattering attentiveness. 'He worries about my living alone and just likes to reassure himself that I've got back safely.'

'And I bet he sometimes leaves messages for you at the places you say you're planning to be.'

Kalera tipped up her small chin. 'Most women find it romantic to know that a man is thinking about her when she's not around. It works both ways, you know. Stephen always lets me know where he'll be and what he's doing...'

'Has he given you one of those incredibly handy pocket planners, yet—so you can carry around all your friends' addresses and phone numbers, and a written diary of all your appointments and things to do, so that whenever he wants to compare schedules you can do it on the spot?'

Kalera thought of the handsome, top-of-the line, leather-bound organiser stamped with her initials which had been Stephen's first gift. She had been touched that he had obviously noticed that she carried a cheap spiral notebook in her handbag as a memory-jogger, tearing off the pages as she went, though was slightly embarrassed at the expensiveness of the gift so early in their relationship.

'Yes, and it's been very useful,' she said, choosing to forget the uncomfortable sense of obligation which had led her firmly to refuse the clothes and jewellery that Stephen had tried to shower her with during the remainder of their courtship, instead restricting him to the traditional tokens of flowers and food.

Duncan wisely accepted her clipped comment as a warning that the subject was closed, but left her with one final dig.

'Given the business he's in, I'm surprised he didn't give you an electronic organiser, but I guess on those things it's too easy to erase entries without a trace. A handwritten diary is usually much more revealing, not to mention accessible, to the casual browser...'

She fulminated over the unsubtle slur, but held her tongue as they worked steadily on through the latter part of the afternoon and through the disruptive clatter of people departing for the day.

As the exodus dwindled to a trickle, Duncan went out to investigate a noisy game of slam-dunk waste-paper basketball going on in the hall.

'What's the matter with you people?' she heard him bellow. 'What is this, a sports stadium? Don't you folks have homes to go to?'

'Yeah, but we don't get paid to play basketball there,' Kalera heard an irreverent voice respond.

'Since it's after five you're not getting paid here, either. No team in the world would hire that lame aiming arm of yours anyway, Digby. Go find somewhere else to humiliate yourself. There're still people *trying* to get work done around here.'

'Try harder,' said someone else, to great guffaws, for

it was a standard phrase of Duncan's if anyone complained that something couldn't be done.

'Aw, c'mon Mr Royal; woncha let Duncan come out to play?' another voice whined.

'Leave the little tyke alone. He's probably still sore that he missed the final free throw the last time he played and lost his team the game...'

Kalera sighed as the challenge lingered in the air, and sure enough there followed a long series of scuffling sounds and numerous muffled thumps and shouts and then a whooping sound of victory. She hid a smile when Duncan returned, slicking back his ruffled black mane, a faint sheen of perspiration on his brow, his chest heaving slightly under his T-shirt.

'I thought you went out there to break it up, not to encourage their unruliness,' she said, handing him another rejection letter to sign.

He met her chiding gaze with a rueful grin. 'If you can't join 'em, beat 'em,' he said, signing with an extravagant flourish.

'One day you're going to be goaded into a challenge you can't win,' she told him.

'I'm as gracious in defeat as I am in victory,' he said, and laughed at her incredulous look. 'All right, so I rage and sulk and throw things...but I'm quick to get over it.'

And so he was, she mused. His tantrums were always brief because there was invariably another idea bubbling up from the depths of his genius to seize hold of his imagination and divert his boundless energies into setting himself a fresh challenge.

The broad band of blue sky outside the tinted window had turned to rose and then to red-gold and then deep indigo before Duncan finally looked at his watch and threw down his pen. 'Goodness, is it that time already?'

'How time flies when you're having fun,' said Kalera drily as she placed the last of the—to her, incomprehensible—'Janet and John' files for Bryan Eastman into the safe-quality lockable drawer in Duncan's desk and handed him the key.

As far as she could see, most of what they had done tonight could have easily waited until the next morning and once Duncan had found out that she didn't have a date with Stephen for him to ruin it had only been his stubborn refusal to admit to his ulterior motive that made him insist that they work this late. At least she felt she had gained some kind of victory in their subtle battle of wills by pretending to be oblivious to the passage of time, forcing him to be the first to cry a halt, but now her rumbling stomach betrayed the fact that it was well past her usual dinner time.

'Hungry?'

In view of her audible digestive system a reply was unnecessary, she thought grumpily, so she countered with a wary question of her own. 'Are we finished?' she queried, in case he merely intended suggesting a break to send out to his favourite restaurant to deliver them a gourmet meal.

Although she had accepted the perk as no less than her due whenever they had worked long hours in her pre-engagement days, now the idea of sharing an exquisitely prepared culinary experience for two in the hushed confines of the deserted office suddenly seemed dangerously intimate. Although there were doubtless still a few other night owls scattered through Labyrinth's network of offices working their own form of glide time, she felt very much alone with Duncan—on his turf and his terms.

Duncan was looking at her with that slightly dreamy, absorbed look of concentration that made her scalp tingle and her skin feel too tight for her body. A look that shared secrets and probed beneath the calm, practical façade which she had adopted to protect herself from an unpredictable world. It beckoned to rebel elements in her nature which she'd thought she had safely subdued but which were showing a nasty tendency to slip their leash and make a mockery of her efforts to embark on a serene life of placid contentment with the man of her choice.

'I guess so—as far as work is concerned, anyway.' Now his deep, gravelly voice seemed to have developed the ability to insinuate itself into her pores and set up a sympathetic vibration along her nerves that made her quiver like a tuning fork.

He stood up and switched off the desk lamp which had augmented the overhead lighting. 'Come on.' He hooked up the battered black leather bomber jacket from the back of his chair with a casual finger and slung it over his shoulder. 'You must be tired as well as hungry by now. I'll take you out for a bite to eat before you drive home—it's the least I can do when you've been such a trooper. I can ring the brasserie across the road for a reservation—'

'Oh, no.' She shook her head so violently that a hairpin dislodged from the sleek French twist and a feather-fine wisp of slippery gold hair drifted down over her breast. She hurriedly scooped it up and repositioned the pin. She *was* feeling light-headed but she had an inkling that it wasn't from hunger! Murky suspicion swam up from the depths of her brain as she mentally pictured the small, trendy restaurant with its romantic, candlelit tables—mostly for two. No one could expect to get in there on Friday night...unless he already *had* a reservation. 'Really, it's not necessary.'

'Actually, it is. Under union rules I *have* to provide you with a meal when your working hours are extended beyond twelve without at least twenty-four hours' notice.'

Kalera, who hadn't even known that she belonged to a union, regarded him with thinly veiled disbelief.

'I really don't feel like eating out.'

'Neither do I,' he said, swiftly conquering a flare of

impatience. He had waited this long; he could endure the torment of her wilful ignorance a little longer. 'But we both need food, preferably with something more nourishing than a snack or greasy take-away, and I certainly don't feel like scratching around in the kitchen at this hour…'

'Well, I do,' she said contrarily. 'I've got a well-stocked fridge and once I get home it won't take me long to whip up something hot and filling—'

'Mmm, that sounds like a wonderful idea!' said Duncan, seizing on her words with frank delight. 'I can't remember the last time anyone offered me any genuine home cooking—the jaded café society set seems to prefer eating out. Why don't you leave first, and I'll follow you home in my car…?'

Astounded by his audacity, Kalera opened her mouth to protest that she hadn't been issuing an invitation.

'Harry used to boast about what a good cook you were,' he continued confidingly. 'Did you know that your recipes were part of his golf-coaching technique? When I was rampaging through the rough and tearing my way from bunker to bunker Harry used to try and calm me down between shots by telling me about the exotic dishes you'd cooked up from some new book or other. He used to get quite poetic about it. Harry certainly loved his food.'

Kalera smiled at the amusing glimpse into their singular friendship. 'He did, didn't he?' Her defences slipped another notch. 'He always bought me a cookbook on our anniversary,' she remembered.

'Your Harry was a very subtle man.'

'Do you think so?' She felt a little jolt of surprise at his undoubted admiration. As far as she was concerned Harry, although quiet and thoughtful, had always been a very straightforward person. 'He gave me cookbooks because he knew I enjoyed trying new recipes; what's so subtle about that?'

'He gave you cookbooks because *he* liked to eat exotic foods and didn't like to cook.' Duncan grinned. 'Dear, unassuming Harry was one of the most astute judges of people I've ever met—I take my hat off to his magnificent ability to quietly get his own way while keeping everyone else around him happily preoccupied with their lesser lot!'

Thirty minutes later Kalera was looking at Duncan making himself comfortably at home in her kitchen and wondering how on earth she had been persuaded to change her mind. Or *had* she changed her mind?

Talk about people who were astute at getting their own way!

CHAPTER SEVEN

'IT'LL have to be something quick and simple,' she reiterated for the third time in as many minutes, opening the fridge and removing an air-tight container of cooked pasta shells and a packet of bacon.

'The simple things in life are always the best,' quoted the man who epitomised the dictionary definition of complexity.

His aura of fatigue had been shed along with his well-used bomber jacket the moment he stepped over her threshold and now he looked disturbingly lively as his enquiring mind conducted an inventory of her possessions, investigating the contents of the set of pottery canisters on the counter and unashamedly perusing the stack of mail she had collected from the letter-box as they'd come in.

He paused in his snooping, his eyes flicking over her high-waisted green skirt and the yellow cotton shirt which had started the day so crisp and smart but which now felt as limp and clammy as warm lettuce against her skin. The weather had been very muggy and the house felt uncomfortably hot and stuffy after being shut up all day.

Kalera usually let down her hair as soon as she got home from work, both literally and figuratively, and changed into something loose and casual, but it would definitely be sending the wrong message if she excused herself with that old cliché about slipping into something more comfortable! She would just have to suffer the discomfort of her prim office armour until he had gone, she thought as she put a pan on the stove to heat and assembled the rest of her ingredients.

'Anything I can do to help?'

'No—yes.' She changed her mind at the thought of him being free to hover about and stare at her in that distracting fashion. Better to give him an occupation—something that would keep his eyes and hands busy.

'You can dice the onion and the rasher of bacon while I do the red pepper and tomatoes,' she ordered, handing him a chopping board and a knife.

He didn't turn a hair at being given the unpleasant half of the job. 'With pleasure, ma'am,' he said, joining her at the bench instead of retreating to the kitchen table, which was what she had intended.

Unexpectedly, the pleasure proved to be hers as she watched him from the corner of her eye, and noted the slightly clumsy way he handled the weighty chef's knife. She responded to his humorous patter and pestering of questions about what they were doing with a faint air of superiority. So there was *something* at which Mr Genius wasn't automatically brilliant, she thought smugly.

'I take it you don't do a lot of cooking yourself,' she murmured, when he swore roundly at the bits of bacon which were balling into a sticky clump on the stainless-steel blade.

'I can cook a superb steak,' he defended himself, peeling off the streaky mess. 'And I've been told that my salad is to die for!'

She could just imagine one of his wafer-thin models batting her false eyelashes at him and massaging his ego with her simpering flattery. 'I wouldn't place any credence on the opinions of any of your Date-Me Barbies. They all look as if a stick of celery is their idea of culinary excellence.'

It was his turn to be smug. 'Do I take it you don't approve of my consorting with beautiful dollybirds?'

'You can date anyone you like,' she said, chopping furiously.

'No; I can't—that's the problem,' he murmured. He shifted his stance as he reached for the onion and his bare arm brushed against her shoulder. He cast her a sidelong glance as she edged away. 'Don't worry, Kalera, I do know the difference between a Barbie doll and a real woman.'

'I'm so glad!'

He grinned at her sarcasm. 'Barbie dolls are for playing—real women are for serious loving…'

Like Terri Prior? Was she his definition of a *real woman*? Kalera brooded. Their loving certainly had been serious enough to break up one marriage, even if it had failed to lead to another.

Maybe it had turned out that the illicit thrill of a secret affair had generated most of the excitement in their relationship, or maybe the burden of their collective guilt had made it impossible to start a new life together. Or maybe Duncan was so gun-shy of commitment that unattainability was his chief defining quality of a 'real woman'…

'Hell and damnation, that stings!'

The onion had taken its acid toll and Duncan scrubbed his streaming eyes with the bottom edge of his T-shirt, unselfconsciously flashing a tanned strip of hard belly neatly bisected by the silky streak of black hair between his navel and the top of his button-fly jeans.

'You're just grinding it in deeper; you should let the tears do their proper job,' Kalera advised, trying not to notice the ripple of satiny skin across his corrugated abdominal muscles as he rubbed the white cotton across his face.

'I'll have you know you're the only woman who can do this to me,' he said, letting the T-shirt drop and blinking furiously to clear his vision.

'Make you chop onions?' she mocked.

His bloodshot eyes captured hers. 'Make me cry.'

In the breathless little silence that followed, the sudden spit of hot olive oil in the frying-pan was a welcome distraction. Turning away, Kalera blindly shovelled in the chopped vegetables and sautéed them with fierce concentration. When they began to brown, she quickly added the pasta just long enough to heat through, and stirred in a sprinkling of the grated Parmesan cheese that she kept in the freezer. The steam from the pan added to the discomfort caused by her snug skirt and stifling tights and she surreptitiously unbuttoned the top two buttons of her blouse, hoping to improve the air circulation over her heated skin.

Since she had determined to treat the meal with the utmost casualness they ate at the kitchen table and after her initial hunger pangs were satisfied Kalera found herself fighting a losing battle against the growing tension which gradually stifled their desultory conversation. Even when her eyes were lowered to her plate she was aware of every bite that Duncan took, every shift of his legs under the table, every dip and tilt of his dark head and flex of his fingers against the tall glass of iced water, which was all she had to offer him to drink.

'This is delicious!' Duncan's sigh of satisfaction forced her to look up to acknowledge his compliment. She watched the fork slide between his lips and the motion of his mouth as he savoured the flare of flavours on his tongue. He chewed slowly, making a bio-mechanical process seem like a sensual act of erotic enjoyment, and when he washed down his swallow of food with a sip of water the gloss of moisture left on his lower lip made Kalera want to lean over and lick it off.

Unnerved by the pang of sexual aggression, she flushed when a piece of pasta slipped off her suspended fork and fell back onto her plate, splashing a little of the cheesy sauce onto her forearm. Unthinkingly she scooped it up with her finger and popped it into her

mouth, a social solecism that she would never have
dreamed of committing if she had been dining with
Stephen.

She cast a sheepish look across the table and froze,
finger in mouth, at Duncan's smouldering expression.
His eyes were black as jet and hot with arousal as he
watched her jerkily release her finger. His lips parted
and his tongue reflexively circled the inner rim of his
mouth, and she knew that he was reliving, as she was,
those fraught moments back at his office.

'You have a unique and very unforgettable taste,' he
said huskily, indicating that his thoughts were reaching
even further back. His eyes dipped to the open V of her
blouse and Kalera felt a tiny trickle of perspiration shim-
mer down between her breasts. 'Sometimes I wake up
in the morning with it so vividly on my tongue that I
roll over, expecting you to be still lying there beside me,
all drowsy and damp with my loving…'

Oh, yes…!

A wild craving leapt in Kalera's blood, clawing for
freedom, but the sound of the telephone ringing in the
hall caged the reckless response before it was uttered.
Her fork clattered onto her plate and with an inarticulate
cry she fled to answer it.

Duncan's head dropped into his hands and he uttered
a thick curse of bitter frustration. Dammit, he had almost
had her. Now she would have time to gather her defences and would be more wary of him than ever.

He prepared himself for the worst, but it was still a
crushing blow when she came back a few minutes later,
the pale oval of her face flushed with shame, her lips
reddened by the indentation of her teeth.

'Stephen,' he guessed, his voice flattened into harsh-
ness by his rigid grip on his emotions. 'I told you he'd
be checking up on you. Did you tell him we were eating?'

She shook her head as she picked up her plate and

took it over to the sink, scraping the rest of her rapidly cooling meal into the waste disposal.

'I think you'd better go.'

His hands clenched beside his plate, his eyes sullen with hostility as they bored into her slender back. 'I haven't finished my pasta yet.'

She clattered her plate into the sink and spun around, her hips pressing back into the hard edge of the bench. 'Please, just go!'

'Did he tell you to say that? Was he furious with you for feeding me? Did he threaten to come over to make sure I was gone?'

'No!' She felt his angry disbelief pulsing at her in physical waves and burst out, 'For goodness' sake—I didn't even tell him you were here!'

She clapped her hands to her hot cheeks and Duncan kicked out of his chair, startled understanding dawning in his eyes.

'And now you're afraid of what will happen if he finds out?' His voice gentled as he moved towards her.

His misunderstanding only poured salt into the wound. 'No, it's not that—' She tried to curl away from him as he approached but he caught her shoulder, pressing her back against the sink.

'I don't even know why I did it,' she said miserably.

Duncan's forefinger curled under her chin and lifted it so that she was forced to meet the steady challenge of his gaze.

'Yes, you do.' His quiet certainty burned like a brand into her consciousness.

'We were just having a meal,' she denied.

'A man and a woman innocently enjoying each other's company,' he agreed softly. He had a gift for making a chaste phrase sound ineffably wicked.

His thumb pressed into the tiny indentation in the middle of her chin, tugging minutely on her lower lip. 'Only it wasn't entirely innocent, was it, Kalera?'

'We weren't *doing* anything,' she blurted feverishly.

His eyes grew slumberous. 'But we wanted to,' he murmured, his hand moving to cup her smooth cheek, encompassing it from jaw to temple, the heel of his palm curving under the angle of her jaw. 'We wanted to do this...' His thumb dragged across her parted mouth, smearing moisture along her lips.

'And we wanted to do this...' He bent his head and fitted his mouth briefly against hers, then again, harder, crushing her lips and darting his tongue between them to sip at her liquid heat.

'And most of all,' he whispered, his mouth still touching hers, his lips caressing her with every word, 'we wanted to do this...'

The force of his third kiss arched her head back and his hand trailed down her exposed throat, over the rumpled opening of her blouse, to settle heavily over the breast pocket of her shirt, his fingers contracting as he ground his palm into the warm mound of flesh. Her eyes fluttered shut at the implosion of blissful excitement. Under the limp cotton of her shirt the fine lace of her bra was a fragile barrier that couldn't hide the firming of her nipple and he found it instinctively with his gliding thumb, circling and scraping at the tight bud with his thumbnail, drawing it out into throbbing sensitivity. His teeth sank into her lip, eating her tiny, helpless moan as his other arm snaked around her waist, pulling her sharply away from the bench and into his body, his hand slanting down over the back of narrow skirt to cup her buttock, kneading the soft globe with imperious fingers, his denim-clad knee rubbing against her flank.

Overwhelmed by the violent storm of physical sensations, Kalera relinquished herself to mindless pleasure, her hands running under his T-shirt to stroke over the taut skin that had tempted her earlier, tracking his ribcage and skimming up over the bunched muscles to play with the soft, springy hair on his chest.

He grunted as her fingers clenched in the luxuriant thicket, her knuckles scraping his flat nipples, the rumbling sound trapped in his chest by the sealing of their mouths. His hand contracted on her bottom, lifting her higher against him so that the centres of their bodies fitted so tightly together she could feel the studs of his jeans grating against her pelvic bone. His mouth was savagely intent on hers as he suddenly shifted his weight, his undulating hips nudging her backwards until her shoulder-blades struck the cool smoothness of sheet metal. Her eyes flew open and she realised that he had laid her against the door of the refrigerator to free his hands for more sinful roving.

He tilted his head, his face filling her vision as he slanted his mobile mouth for greater access, his closed eyes making her aware of the thin-skinned delicacy of his eyelids and the way his dark brows had rumpled into his forehead as if he were in great pain, prompting a fierce surge of tenderness to soften the raw physicality of her response and turn it into something infinitely more threatening to her emotional safety.

But as his denim-clad thigh thrust between hers and his hands raked open the buttons of her blouse she couldn't remember why she should care. The mingled scent of their heated bodies was a heady bouquet in her nostrils and went like wine to her head, so that when Duncan broke the endless kiss to curse over a lone snagged button a bubble of husky laughter escaped her throat.

Goaded by the sexy sound, he lost patience and ripped her blouse open, thrusting his hands into the stretch lace cups of her bra and dragging them down to expose her swollen, brown-tipped breasts.

He bent his head and ran his tongue around the puckered rims, finishing with a brief, rasping flick across the rigid crowns. Kalera's head fell back against the fridge, her shoulders slumping, her hands sliding down to his compact waist where her nails curled convulsively into the firm resilience of his skin.

'When I was sucking your fingers,' he told her thickly, 'I was fantasising that they were these…' He blew lightly across the responsive peaks and watched her breasts quiver with the tremulous rise of her ribcage, her nipples visibly reacting to the moist stroke of air. 'I remember how much you enjoyed me playing with them, how you leaned over me and fed them to my lips like ripe berries…'

She shivered wildly. 'Oh, please…'

'Please what?' His fingers surrounded her breasts, his thumbs pushing the pouting nipples up towards his mouth as he slowly sank to his knees in front of her. 'Please please you? Of course I will—that's my mission in life, darling,' he vowed as he enveloped her in a lashing wet fire that made her bones crumble and her flesh melt.

Lost in a carnal world where everything was subordinate to the pleasure-giving caress of his mouth, Kalera reached flashpoint with stunning speed. Suddenly the aching delight that she was experiencing became shot with feverish urgency. Her hands cupped Duncan's head, her fingers weaving sensuously into his hair as one slender thigh rubbed up and down his side, her back flexing to rock her hips insistently against his chest.

Duncan's hands tightened on her restless flanks, sliding up to her hips to anchor her against the fridge as he rose back to his full height.

'Oh, no,' he growled, letting her feel the hard bulge between his legs jutting against her belly. 'Not this time…this time I don't have to be noble and restrained. This time, when I give you an orgasm I want to be inside you…'

This time. The phrase ricocheted around inside Kalera's turgid brain, exploding her sensual trance, triggering a rising panic as he continued triumphantly, 'This

time we make love as equals, and we have names—
Kalera and Duncan. And this time there'll be no ghost
joining us in the bed…!'

Ghost. He was talking about Harry, as if the lingering
spirit of her past love had been the only stumbling block
to their tumbling headlong into a scorching affair.

But he was wrong, horribly wrong, for there were a
host of other very good reasons why it was a very bad
idea—the crucial one being emphatically no ghost…

As if she had uttered his name the telephone began to
ring again, a shrill cry of reproach from the other room.
Kalera's head began to turn towards the sound and
Duncan's hand slammed into the fridge beside her head,
the thick column of his arm blocking her view of the
door.

'No, dammit!' At her flinch his shout dropped to a
mere yell as he caged her with his other arm. 'Don't
answer it!'

'I have to—'

She frantically tugged up her bra, wincing as it compressed her tender nipples, and shakily buttoned her
shirt.

'No, you don't. It's not illegal to ignore a ringing
phone.'

The electronic burr seemed louder with every repetition.

'But it might be important,' she protested, trying to
duck under his arms.

He lowered them to hip-level, trapping her even more
effectively. 'It's Prior again, isn't it?' His searching gaze
found confirmation in her anxious face. 'You know it
is—so does that mean he always calls more than once
when you've been out late?'

How could she have let Stephen's hitherto trivial little
habit slip her mind? Because when Duncan was kissing
her she didn't *have* a mind!

'If he realises he's forgotten to tell me something—'

'And to make certain that you haven't gone out again,' he interpreted grimly.

It was true that Stephen's reasons were invariably petty and he never chatted long, but she had flattered herself that it was out of affection that he wanted to hear the sound of her voice again. 'I'm sure that's not why—'

'Of course it is. He's testing you, Kalera, trying to control you by remote, and you're letting him get away with it. I bet if it was me calling you all the time you'd soon tell me where to get off!'

How long was the wretched phone going to continue ringing?

'*You're* not my fiancé,' she retorted. 'I only work for you...' Her words trailed off as his nostrils flared.

'Only? *Only?* Oh, that isn't *only* all that you do for me, Kalera...' He leaned forward just far enough for his erection to tease the fabric of her taut skirt.

Kalera swallowed. 'Look—he knows I'm here. If I don't answer he'll ask me about it tomorrow—'

'You can tell him you were in the shower.'

'I don't shower in the evenings.'

'You did the night you slept with me. When you came to bed your skin was all soft and clean and soap-scented. For the next few weeks, every time I had a shower I washed myself all over with that very same cake of soap...'

Her hands clutched protectively at the front of her blouse.

'Stop it! Just stop it! And let me answer my own damned phone!'

His eyes gleamed with satisfaction at her rare flash of temper. 'Maybe Steve won't be happy until his suspicions are confirmed. Maybe he figures that if he calls often enough the law of averages will apply and one night he'll catch you out when your lover accidentally picks up the phone.' His arms dropped away and he stepped back. 'Maybe *I* should answer it and put him out of his misery...'

He headed for the door and after a frozen moment Kalera burst into action.

'No!' Aghast, she grabbed at the back of his T-shirt and hauled on it, not knowing whether he really meant to carry out his threat or was merely tormenting her with the possibility. There was a brief tug of war over the stretching T-shirt, in the midst of which she became aware that the ringing had finally stopped.

With a sob of relief she let go and Duncan wheeled back, the merciless kitchen lighting exposing the depth of his anger.

'Let that be a lesson to you,' he told her ruthlessly. 'If you think you feel guilty now, wait until he *really* gets to work on you—you'll be apologising for drawing breath without his permission!'

She took a sharp breath, furious at him for manipulating her emotions simply to illustrate a point. 'It'll be different when we're married—'

'The hell it will!' he exploded incredulously, naked fury crackling out of every pore. 'After what happened between us just now you must have realised you can't possibly go ahead with this farcical engagement!'

His words merely confirmed her painful suspicion that what had been for her a spontaneous loss of control had for Duncan been a carefully planned and executed assault on her virtue. She had been tested and had failed miserably. But that didn't mean that she should give up and let passion rule her life, she told herself fiercely. Giving up the dreams that she had held since girlhood for the sake of the fleeting pleasures of the moment would be by far the greater failure!

'I don't see why not,' she said, straightening her slim shoulders.

'Because you don't bloody love him, that's why!' he yelled hoarsely.

'That's your opinion.' She held steady, as she always did, in the face of his flamboyant wrath.

'It's not an opinion, it's an obvious fact!' he grated. 'Tell me, would you have carried on like this with me if I'd been around when you were engaged to Harry?'

Her face went white, then red, as if he had struck her.

'Let's leave Harry out of this,' she said, almost choking on her outrage. She had finally worked out—idiot that she was—that whenever Duncan was trying to talk her into doing something that went against the grain he invoked the spirit of her dead husband to soften her up and use her feelings to distract her from the issue at hand.

'No, of course you wouldn't have,' he answered for her. 'You stopped looking at other men when you found Harry. I never even had a chance with you while he was alive. But with Stephen it's different—whatever else you feel for him, he obviously doesn't excite you sexually. If he did you wouldn't be using me to provide you with your orgasms—'

Her hand cracked across his cheek, the force of the unexpected blow snapping his head to one side and knocking the insulting words back on his tongue. By the time he had recovered she had marched to the front door and thrown it open with a crash, the red mist of rage blurring her vision making it momentarily difficult to see him as he trailed after her.

'Get out!'

He emerged from the red veil moving with deliberate slowness, sullenly manipulating his injured jaw. 'Does Steve know you pack a punch like that, or am I the only man who can provoke you to such violent passion?'

As a blind shot across her bows it was devastatingly effective. Thank God it was Friday night. By the time she had to face him again she would have been able to put the whole humiliating episode into its proper perspective.

'Go!' She pointed out into the darkness and instantly regretted her overly dramatic gesture when an irrepressible spark of humour smouldered to life in the brooding depths of his eyes.

'You're so cute when you're acting dominant,' he mocked as he drew level. 'Like a fairy fluffed up on steroids. Aren't you going to tell me never to darken your door again?'

She gritted her teeth. 'Don't tempt me!'

'Why? Afraid you won't be able to resist...*again*?'

'If you want me to be at work on Monday don't— say—another—*word*,' she said, cyanide dripping from every carefully articulated syllable.

He threw up his hands. 'All right, all right, I'm going.' He ran lightly down the steps, turning at the bottom to look back up at her slender figure, silhouetted in the doorway, unable to resist claiming the last word.

''Night, darling.' His voice was smoky in the gloom. 'If you have an urgent need for my—er—*services* over the weekend, you know how to find me—I'm number four on the speed dial of your phone. I see that poor Prior only rates a lowly nine!'

She might have known his offer to open a few windows for her while she checked through her mail had had an ulterior motive. He must have made the most of his brief opportunity to poke around, as he had in the kitchen. Trust him to notice such a petty detail!

'That's only because Harry put you on the infernal thing and I don't know how to change the listings,' she yelled after his retreating back. 'I'd soon wipe you off if only I could find the instructions!'

She slammed the door on his answering chuckle and a few moments later heard the potent throb of the McLaren diminish into the night.

Why did she let him provoke her like that? He never used to be able to get under her skin but now he was embedded there like a troublesome burr. Thank goodness it was dark, otherwise the whole neighbourhood would have been treated to the sight of that quiet widow from number 43, screaming like a fishwife from her doorstep at that handsome, black-haired devil with the foreign car, and her engaged to that nice blond chap...

Oh, yes, Kalera could well imagine how the gossip over neighbourly cups of tea would go, and as usual the basic facts would get distorted as they twined around the local grapevine.

Darkness notwithstanding, maybe she *had* better mention Duncan's visit to Stephen, just in case he heard it later from another source...

CHAPTER EIGHT

KALERA expected to have a dreadful night, tossing and turning and berating herself for her appalling weakness and lack of moral fibre, but once she put her head on the pillow she went out like a light and woke the next morning feeling magnificently alive and wonderfully energetic.

She had delegated the day for cleaning and sorting, aware that at some vague point in the future she would have to decide what possessions she would carry forth into her new life with Stephen and not wanting to be rushed over the choosing.

Since none of her undistinguished furniture fitted in with the elegant designer decor of his home it was only her personal belongings that would require packing up, but there were many books, papers, photos and mementos from her marriage with Harry that she needed to look through and decide whether to take with her or store.

Harry had been a fiend for jigsaw puzzles and there were dozens of them crammed in the wardrobe in the spare room. The two of them had spent many a happy hour taking alternate turns on the most challenging puzzles and although Kalera doubted that Stephen's sophisticated tastes ran to such simple entertainment it occurred to her that Michael might be old enough to show an interest in some of the simpler versions featuring trains, cars and maps of the world. Stephen hadn't been very informative about his son's character but she did know that he was very bright for his age and already reading well above the normal six-year-old level. He might need help on the jigsaws, but Kalera thought that working on puzzles together would be a good way of alleviating the inevitable awkwardness of their step-relationship.

Imbued with the restless vitality with which she had awoken, by late morning Kalera had done most of her cleaning chores, discarded some old financial files and decided which puzzles she would give away to the local old people's home. After lunch, she decided virtuously, she would wash the windows. Last time Stephen was in her living room she had noticed him raise an eyebrow at the haze on the glass ranch-slider which looked out onto her flower garden. He had been too polite to say anything but, knowing how immaculately kept his own house was—albeit by a paid housekeeper—she had been attuned to his faint emanations of disapproval. It was just that she had been kept so busy at Labyrinth since she had given her notice that the last thing she wanted to do when she got home in the evenings was physical labour!

She was wavering between making herself a sandwich or salad for lunch when Stephen rang to finalise the time he would pick her up for the charity dinner and symphony concert that they were attending that evening. She mentioned her idea about Michael and the jigsaw puzzles and to her disappointment he was noncommittal, the wary reserve that always appeared in his tone when he spoke about his son as much in evidence as ever.

'Since his mother refuses to accept that I'm getting married again the boy is receiving some conflicting messages. Let's not confuse him even more with other demands on his loyalty...'

He always called Michael 'the boy', which Kalera felt was slightly dehumanising. Perhaps it was just his way of distancing himself from the pain of knowing that his son was no longer an integral part of his daily life.

'By the way,' he tacked on diffidently, 'I rang back

last night to ask you what colour corsage you'd like for this evening and you didn't answer—'

The doorbell rang and Kalera padded to answer it in her bare feet, the cordless phone pressed to her ear, listening with a sinking heart as Stephen said jokingly, 'I know Royal is working you like a galley slave but surely you can't have fallen asleep so quickly? You said you were still finishing dinner when we spoke the first time.'

Of *course* he was curious—who wouldn't be? Curiosity was a perfectly natural, healthy human reaction, thought Kalera, swapping the phone to her other ear as she fumbled to turn the heavy deadlock with her favoured hand. In fact, she probably would have asked the same idle question of Stephen if their situations had been reversed.

So why did she feel a deep reluctance to answer?

Last night she had decided in favour of offering him an edited version of Duncan's visit, but now, faced with the daunting task of censoring as she went, she took the coward's way out.

'I guess I must have been in the shower,' she said as she got the door open and, to her horror, found herself staring up into Duncan's wickedly satyric face.

Vivid colour rushed into her cheeks as he mouthed 'hello' with an exaggerated caution and she realised that he had heard her remark and guessed what it meant.

'I let it ring for quite a while—' Stephen was saying in her ear as she quickly tried to shut the door again. Too late; a custom-made, crocodile-skin boot was firmly planted as a door-stop.

'Uh—I was washing my hair…it always takes me ages.' She stepped to one side to block the doorway as Duncan tried to slip past her into the house.

'Are you all right? You sound a bit distracted.'

'Someone's ringing the doorbell; I'd better go and see who it is. It's probably only some sleazy door-to-door salesman trying to palm off something cheap and nasty that nobody in their right mind would want,' she said, aiming the gritty words directly at Duncan. 'Yes, yes—of course I'll be careful, Stephen. Bye!'

'Very smooth,' said Duncan as she flipped off the 'talk' button, and propped the phone on the narrow ceramic pipe that she used as an umbrella stand. 'Do you think he believed you?'

She planted her hands on her hips, and herself squarely in the centre of the doorway.

'What are you doing here?'

He was wearing another pair of jeans, this time white, and a multicoloured woven waistcoat over a collarless white Indian cotton shirt—a striking combination that made Kalera, in her plain blue denims and ribbed pink top, feel very ordinary...but then that was no different from usual!

What *was* different was the way that her heart was knocking in her chest—not with apprehension, but in fizzing anticipation of another stormy clash.

Duncan eased his foot from the door and, when he saw that she wasn't going to budge, composed his handsome face into sober lines.

'I came to say I'm sorry for last night,' he said quietly, with the ease of a man who was as open about his faults as he was frank with the rest of his emotions. 'I lost my temper and said some things that I shouldn't have...rude, crude and hurtful things that you had every right to treat with bitter contempt. I abused your hospitality and sullied a precious memory of sweet rapture by throwing it back in your face as an insult. My only explanation—because I know it's not an excuse—is that I was overwhelmed by genuine, strong feelings that were just too big for me to keep inside...

'I hope you can forgive me and give me another chance—I don't want to lose our friendship...'

Kalera's attention, which had briefly snagged on that 'precious memory of sweet rapture', caught up with what he was saying. She didn't trust him when he was being meek and humble and yet she knew him well enough to recognise when he was truly sincere. That sincerity tugged at her heartstrings, even though she noticed that he wasn't apologising for his deeds, only his words.

She folded her arms across her chest. She had forgiven him so many times in the past for his fiery displays of temperament that perhaps he was justified in thinking that all he had to do was ask.

'I'll think about it.'

His boot edged tentatively back up onto the doorstep. 'Perhaps we could go inside and talk it over—sort out where we go from here...'

Panic flared in her eyes. 'I was just going out.'

His gaze wandered down to where her bare toes curled against the doormat and his mouth twitched at the sight of her frosted pink toenails. 'Like that?'

'I was just about to put my shoes on and get my bag when the phone rang—'

'Where are you going?' He interrupted her earnest efforts to sound convincing. 'Shopping?'

'Why?'

He shrugged. 'Perhaps I could come with you and we can talk at the same time.'

'No, we can't. I'm going over to my parents' place for lunch.' Kalera was getting so good at lying she almost believed herself!

'Oh.' He glanced over at her car, his eyes narrowing thoughtfully. 'I remember meeting them briefly at Harry's funeral,' he murmured. 'Perhaps I can give you a lift. Where do they live?'

'Not far,' she evaded. If she gave him an address he was quite capable of turning up there himself. 'But I want to take my own car. Look—I'll be late if I don't get a move on...' She glanced pointedly at her watch.

He leaned on the door jamb. 'OK. I'll wait here while you get your things.'

Oh, no! 'For God's sake, why?' she blurted.

'My mother drilled into me that a gentleman always walks a lady to her car,' he replied glibly. 'Go on...I promise I won't sneak inside as soon as your back is turned.'

If he suspected her of lying he had just effectively called her bluff.

Trapped, Kalera had no choice but to do as he had bid. If she *had* to go out to get rid of him she might as well turn fiction into fact and play the dutiful daughter, she thought, digging in her handbag for her car keys as she returned to the front door.

Duncan offered his elbow to her and grinned when she responded with a frosty cold shoulder. Not even Stephen was so ridiculously punctilious that he insisted on escorting her to her own car parked in broad daylight on her own property!

Since the house didn't have a lock-up garage her Toyota was parked under the small carport in the driveway and as they approached it Kalera's steps slowed. Now she saw why Duncan had been so anxious to wait outside while she was busy getting ready—her rear tyre was flat! Inwardly steaming, she walked silently around the back of the car and discovered that *both* rear tyres were flat, thus rendering the spare tyre in the boot useless.

'Bad luck.' Duncan crouched down to take a closer look. 'Do you think you might have driven over some nails?'

Kalera looked down at the taut white backside presented to her vision and was very tempted to plant her dainty foot against the straining seam and give a hefty shove.

'Do I *look* that stupid?' She boiled over. 'I'll tell you what I *think*! I *think* that you need a good psychiatrist to cure your Napoleon complex, that's what! I think you're a selfish, egotistical swine who'd murder his own mother to get his own way!'

She took a step forward as Duncan rose to his feet and tried to speak, jabbing him in the chest with her finger in staccato rhythm with her accusing words. 'How dare you think you can get away with a cheap trick like this? I'm sick of your pathetic games of one-upmanship and sordid attempts at manipulation. And this—this *juvenile* behaviour is just the last *straw*—'

'Uh, Mrs Martin? Kalera?' Interrupted in mid-flow, Kalera swung around to see her neighbour from two doors down urging her angelic-faced eight-year-old twin sons up the driveway towards them.

'Sorry to interrupt,' the woman said awkwardly, her gaze swinging from Kalera's red face to Duncan's annoyed one, and then to the car behind them. She sighed. 'But then I guess you might be able to figure out why we've come... Go on Jeremy—Shane.' She urged the twins in front of her and gave them a sharp nudge when they remained silent.

Mystified, Kalera pinned on a limp smile. Her genuine affection for children had put her on easy terms with most of those in the neighbourhood, and these two were no exception.

'What is it, guys?'

'We're sorry for letting down your car tyres, Mrs Martin!' the pink-cheeked cherubs chirped in unison, and Kalera's jaw fell open.

'They were just imitating something they'd seen on television; they didn't really appreciate that they were doing something very naughty,' their mother said hastily, misinterpreting Kalera's glassy-eyed stare. 'They were up at the crack of dawn this morning playing cops and robbers in the front yard and I was *so* pleased they were letting my husband and I sleep in that I didn't think to check what they were doing. Not that I imagined they'd get up to anything like this! And I'm afraid it wasn't just you—they let down tyres all the way up the street. When they told me I was just floored!'

'Boys will be boys,' murmured Duncan, when it seemed that Kalera was going to remain embarrassingly speechless.

'Since I have two more under five that doesn't exactly reassure me,' said the woman wryly, relaxing under his sympathetic smile. 'I'm *awfully* sorry. We can't afford to pay for a garage to come and fix all the cars but Don has gone out to hire an air cylinder and he'll reinflate all the tyres to the proper pressure as soon as he can...'

When the trio had trooped on towards their next confession, Duncan turned to Kalera with an ironic tilt of his black brows.

'You were saying...?'

'Well, the way you've been carrying on lately you can't blame me for thinking it might have been you,' she said sulkily.

'You were right on the money about it being juvenile behaviour,' he responded, with a graciousness that made her feel even more surly when she recalled her volley of accusations.

She squared her shoulders and said grudgingly, 'I suppose you want an apology.'

'It does rather seem like the day for them,' he said cheerfully. 'But, don't worry—you'll have plenty of time to compose one on the way.'

'The way?'

He indicated his beloved McLaren, slunk at the kerb. 'It looks like I'll have to give you that lift after all, doesn't it? You mustn't disappoint your parents by not turning up for lunch!'

Since Kalera had been disappointing her parents all her life, first as a colicky baby whose failure to thrive on breast-feeding had deprived Silver Donovan of the full satisfaction of her 'earth-mother' phase, then as a shy child, introspective teenager and stubbornly conservative adult, she was used to fending off their fond fantasies that she would one day 'get in touch with herself' and strike out on some bold, creative endeavour that would utilise her hitherto totally dormant artistic talents.

Therefore it was extremely disconcerting to find herself showered with approval for turning up with Duncan in tow—or, rather, towed *by* Duncan.

'Crystal Dreams?' Duncan murmured, his eyes widening as he pulled up outside her parents' address and read off the swirling letters painted in bright purple along the sagging overhead verandah of the dilapidated wooden building. He double-checked the crooked number above the open door of the shop, sandwiched between a seedy-looking antique store and a vegetarian restaurant, with a retro clothing store displaying a Paisley shirt and red bell-bottoms and a hairdresser's taking up the rest of the small area of strip shopping.

'*This* is your parents' place?' Unlike Stephen's reaction on his first—and last—visit, Duncan's shock held no hint of aversion. Bright with intrigued interest, his eyes rose to the faded upper storey, where a curtain blew out of an open window hung with crystal mobiles, and a profusion of pot plants and wind-chimes joined drying washing on a tiny balcony. His gaze returned to study the artistically arranged crystals, gemstone jewellery displayed cheek-by-jowl in the crammed shop window with Rastafarian beads, homeopathic remedies, New Age books and posters about upcoming Druid festivals, clairvoyants, tarot and psychic readings and gypsy fairs. 'They own the shop—and live here, too?'

'Thanks for the lift,' Kalera said, squirming out of the scooped seat, vainly hoping her lack of answer would deter his curiosity. 'My parents'll drop me home—'

Duncan was already out of the car and halfway across the footpath. 'Your parents are into alternative lifestyles?' He leaned up to the window, peering intently into the chaotic interior, his breath misting the glass. 'Groovy!'

Wild horses wouldn't have stopped him venturing inside to explore the cluttered shelves and stampeding elephants wouldn't have chased him out when Kalera's parents swarmed out from the back room uttering cries of surprised welcome, her mother tall and tanned, her long hair bouncing down her back in a single fat braid and her father stocky and thickly bearded, with a grey-streaked ponytail almost as long as his wife's.

'Sunny! I should have known you'd turn up today— my stars predicted that someone closely related to me would make a special journey on my behalf!' Silver crowed, her long crinkle-cotton dress fluttering as she flung her thin arms out to greet her daughter with a breath-shattering squeeze, her rows of jangling bangles snagging on the silky knit of Kalera's top.

'I only live a couple of kilometres away—I'd hardly classify it as a *journey*,' she said drily, when her mother allowed her to surface for air. 'Hello, Kris.' She submitted to her father's hairy hug, trying to avoid the sight of Duncan's knowing grin as her bluff was exposed.

'Oh, phooey! You're always so literal…astrology is about the *bigger* picture! Tell her what I said, Kris, when I read it last night—I said, I wonder if that means Sunny might turn up tomorrow?'

'That's what she said,' Kris Donovan agreed amiably. Kalera felt her stomach tighten at the slightly unfocussed look in his eyes. Her parents' attitude to soft drugs was another reason that she had separated her life from theirs and created her own set of guiding principles. She loved them but didn't like some of the choices they had made in life. She hoped Kris hadn't left a joint smoking out in the back room. The way her luck was running lately they would be raided and she and Duncan would end up under arrest!

'Sonny?' said Duncan out of the corner of his mouth. 'Do they think their daughter is a son?'

Her mother overheard and laughed. 'That's her name—Sunshine Kalera Donovan…because she was born outside on the grass, a real natural childbirth—at the commune we were living in at the time…' She chattered on with her usual lack of circumspection about Kalera's marvellous sunlit childhood, unfettered by the rules of society or the tyranny of government, or the brainwashing of state education. 'It was only when she decided she had to go to high school that she refused to answer to Sunny and made everyone call her by the middle name that Kris's mother insisted she have. It's a pity, isn't it, because I think Sunshine suits her—don't you?'

They both looked at Kalera, whose mouth was drawn into a little prune of annoyance, and Duncan's voice was silky with amusement as he said, 'Actually, I think moonlight suits her even better…'

Silver laughed again, her blue eyes flirting in approval at his wit. 'You're Duncan, the computer man, aren't you? Kris and I spoke to you at Harry's funeral. Did you come with Sunny, or are you interested in crystal healing?'

'I did come with Kalera,' he said, so gravely that only she was aware of the wicked *double entendre* indicated by the tell-tale flick of muscle at the corner of his mouth. 'But I wouldn't mind finding out a bit about the way your crystals are supposed to work.'

'You mean how they *do* work,' scolded Silver, but Duncan couldn't have said anything better calculated to open the floodgates and soon he and the two Donovans were deep in a discussion of belief versus science, leaving a disgruntled Kalera to serve the customers. All too soon the conversation strayed from psychic healing, astral projection and aura cleansing to more personal matters and she heard Kris being shamelessly pumped for more reminiscences of commune life involving Kalera.

'We get the odd hankering to go back to the old life, don't we, love?' she heard her father say. 'This is the longest time we've stayed in one place since Sun—I mean Kalera—was born. But we're only on a short lease with the shop so we can just pick up and go pretty well whenever we want—maybe load all this stuff into a gypsy caravan and travel the fairs for a few years...'

'What a great idea!'

Kalera imagined Stephen's reaction to seeing his in-laws drive up to his front door for a visit in a rattletrap gypsy caravan, and shuddered. He had been polite but cool to her parents on the few occasions they had met, and she knew that he was relieved that her relationship with them wasn't closer. Duncan, on the other hand, was proving a kindred spirit...so much so that she was aghast to hear Silver proposing to shut up shop so that they could all go to the vegetarian restaurant next door for lunch.

An hour later she sat toying with her sprout salad, listening to her mother tell her what a wonderfully open-minded man she worked for—the man in question wolfing down his aubergine casserole and trying his best not to look smug.

And failing.

'He's so *receptive* to new ideas, I can see that working for him must be intensely *stimulating* to the creative imagination,' Silver expounded over her plate of stir-fried tofu. 'It's such a *pity* that you're not going to stay on there, Sunny...' She heaved a disappointed sigh, and Kalera stopped picking at her salad to regard her in disbelief.

'When I first started there you told me working at Labyrinth would stifle my ''small inner voice'' and the radiation from all those computers would stunt my aura!' she reminded her bluntly.

Silver was unembarrassable. 'Yes, well, *that* was before I got to know Duncan better.' She patted his arm fondly with her heavily be-ringed fingers.

'You only met him an hour ago,' Kalera pointed out, nettled at the ease with which he had insinuated himself.

'Yes, but I could see right away that he had a very healthy aura,' said Silver blithely. 'He's definitely good karma, Sunny...and so very *broad-minded* about things.' Her crowning compliment! 'Much better for you than that stuffy Stephen. I remember when you brought *him* here you were brittle as a stick the whole time in case he took offence at something we said, but look at you now—happy to kick back and just go with the flow...'

That was because she knew the flow was actually an unstoppable torrent, thought Kalera, although it was true she didn't have to worry about Duncan taking offence at her parents' outlandish eccentricities—he was in his perfect element!

She noticed that he had stopped eating, his ears pricking up at the sound of Stephen's name, and a little 'alert' sign switched on in her brain.

'Silver...' she warned.

'Oh, I know, you don't want us to hassle you about it.' Silver flapped her hands. 'It's your life, you live it— but really I can't help thinking that the man is impossibly *dull*. At least Harry, for all he was a bit of a stick-in-the-mud, had a sense of humour and was good for a few laughs. I can't see you having much fun with Stephen— you're both so tiresomely *serious*. I suppose he is sexy in a chilly kind of way, but I can't imagine I'd find him very thrilling in bed—he's far too uptight. Or is great sex the big attraction?'

Kalera flushed, clinging to her temper. 'Silver, I'm going to *marry* him—'

'You ought to move in with him for a while first...see if you still want to stay when the sex stops being such a kick—'

'Stephen can't do that; he has Michael to consider.'

'That's why you *should* move in. At least then you might get a chance to meet the kid! And anyway, what's wrong with him knowing that you're having sex with his father? Kids accept sex as an intrinsic part of life if you treat it as natural and normal and not some dirty secret that should be hidden. You saw Kris and I with lots of different sex partners when you were young and it never bothered you!'

With an effort Kalera managed not to flinch. Her mother really had no idea of just how severely bothered her daughter had been by that casual exhibitionism, or how pressured she had felt to conform when approached for casual sex by other commune members, even when she was still below the age of legal consent.

'You're engaged to Stephen and he still hasn't introduced you to Michael?' Duncan interjected. 'What's he planning to do—wait until you're married and spring you on the boy as his stepmother?'

'No, of course not,' snapped Kalera, who wasn't so certain any more that Stephen didn't intend to do exactly that. But that didn't make him as insensitive as Duncan was implying. 'Terri's making things difficult right now by refusing to allow unaccompanied visits, and Stephen doesn't want to upset Michael by turning him into a tug-of-love child—'

'*Terri's* making it difficult?'

His emphasis stung and her eyes warred with his. Of course, he *would* take his lover's side, she thought nastily.

Fortunately, her father was already meandering off on another conversational track which diverted the brewing conflict, but Kalera was still brooding over Duncan's sneering remark when they left a short time later. She had tried to object when he had chided that she needn't bother her parents for a lift home, but after insisting on paying for their meal—an offer Silver and Kris had accepted with embarrassing alacrity—Duncan was in a position of unassailable strength.

'We mightn't have been able to get you all the way home, anyway,' laughed Kris, putting the seal on his daughter's fate. 'The VW's been conking out on us quite a bit, lately.'

'Interesting people,' said Duncan as they left the re-opened shop.

'So…you were brought up outside the mainstream of society by a couple of radical free-thinkers,' he mused when she didn't respond.

'What's wrong with that?' she snapped, having vowed that she wasn't going to say another word to him. She might find her background embarrassing, but she wasn't ashamed of it.

'Nothing; it just explains some things,' he said, unlocking her door and handing her into the car before swinging in behind the wheel. 'Do you like them—as people, I mean?'

At the last moment Kalera couldn't resist being honest. 'Most of the time, yes. But their love was so freely shared around that I never felt *special*, or intimately connected with them, and they took so little responsibility for me that I doubt they knew I was around a lot of the time. I cope best if I try to think of them just as a screwball couple I know.'

'Difficult?'

'Impossible,' she sighed. 'But, listening to Kris, I don't think they'll be here much longer. As usual they'll get bored with what they're doing and take off to find some new fad or vessel of enlightenment, and I won't hear from them for months—or years.'

'Well, I liked your screwball friends,' Duncan teased, pulling up at a red light. 'And they seemed to like me too. I think we're working on a majority opinion, here: your parents like me, the people who work for me like me—*you* like me! Stephen seems to be the only dissenter...'

Her head jerked around. 'I wonder if your affair with his wife has anything to do with that?' she pondered sarcastically.

The harsh sunlight streamed in through the windscreen, causing his eyes to narrow as he stared straight ahead. 'He doesn't hate my guts because I had an affair with his wife. He hates my guts because he *thinks* I did.'

It took a moment for her to realise what the quiet words implied. Cars roared across the intersection in front of them, adding to the thunder in her head.

'Are you saying you never had an affair with Terri?' she demanded hoarsely, willing him to look at her and yet afraid of what she would see when he did.

His fingers flexed and curled back around the compact steering wheel, his profile taking on a hawkish intensity.

'Oh, yes, we had an affair,' he admitted with a deep-throated passion that was like a sharp punch over the heart. 'When we were both young, single and free we were crazy about each other for a short while. But that was over before she got engaged to Stephen. I never touched her after that. She was in love with Stephen and as far as I was concerned she was my friend's wife. My relationship with Terri was just that—pure friendship—and I felt very sorry for her when the marriage started to turn sour because of Stephen's suffocating jealousies...'

But sympathy could sometimes easily be mistaken for something else, Kalera thought, not only by Stephen, but Terri, too—if not before, then perhaps in the vulnerable aftermath of the break-up of the marriage...

'But surely he must have had some reason to feel jealous in the first place...'

Duncan's head turned at last, his expression a volatile mixture of bitterness, anger, resignation and contempt. '*Yes*, he had a reason—his own obsession! He always

did have a controlling personality but it pushed him to
want *absolute* control in his marriage. He was always
demanding to know where Terri had been, expecting her
to account for every moment of time she spent away
from him, objecting to anything that took her attention
away from him—job, friends—both male and female—
shopping, family, hobbies…'

Kalera swallowed. This was all beginning to sound
creepily familiar!

Duncan's eyes went back to the road.

'And when he couldn't verify any of his ridiculous
suspicions and Terri turned to me for advice and help
he latched onto me as the most enviable and convenient
target for his mistrust. That way he didn't have to admit
he was in the wrong,' he said grimly, sliding the car into
gear and accelerating away the instant the light went
green, driving them both back into their seats. He drove
with a controlled aggression the rest of the way through
the suburbs, painting a vivid word-picture of a man
caught up in a spiral of self-deceit.

'He destroyed a friendship and a marriage for the sake
of a delusion. Towards the end Terri even caught him
reading her diary and opening her letters, following her
in his car, and coming home at odd times of the day to
try and catch us out.

'She left him because she couldn't cope, and he
blamed me for that, too. Anyone but himself and his own
self-destructive urges. Terri told him that she still loved
him but she wouldn't go back to him until he agreed to
get professional help. Instead he chose to spite them both
by getting a divorce, but he still can't let her go—even
now, with you in his life… He won't admit either his
own culpability, or the fact that he still loves her…'

He had stopped the car and in a blur of humiliation
Kalera managed to comprehend that she was home. Soon
she would be safe from this relentless emotional on-
slaught. She fumbled her seat belt undone, scrabbling

for the door handle with a trembling hand, and Duncan's arm shot across to detain her, trapping her against the seat-back.

'Open your eyes, Kalera,' he urged fiercely. 'He's sick—and instead of getting treatment for his illness he's trying to substitute one obsession for another. It's started already—he's training you to accept his intrusion into every facet of your life—'

His arm was like an iron band across her breasts, the small cockpit of the car chokingly oppressive as Kalera struggled to gather her shattered thoughts. 'He has a *right* to intrude; he's going to be my *husband*.'

Duncan made a rough sound in his throat. 'That's the way he *wants* you to think. I know you need security and that's probably why you're marrying him, but what he's got in mind is a maximum security prison. And with Steve there's no parole for good behaviour!'

'So this is just a friendly warning, right?' Kalera cried, desperate to escape and lick her wounds in private. 'You have no axe to grind, no desire to get revenge for him publicly branding you an adulterer when you're actually as innocent as a newborn babe?'

In her anxiety to get away she knew she had made it sound as if she didn't believe him. But she did—at least she thought the *core* of what he said might be true but that, as usual, he was wildly exaggerating the details to give them the most emotional impact. Stephen was an extremely intelligent man and ran a complex and highly successful business. He might have some emotional problems, but Duncan was making him sound psychotic.

Duncan cursed with vicious fluency. 'I'm breaking a promise to tell you this—I'm *trying* to stop you making a fool of yourself.'

He must mean a promise to Terri, thought Kalera with a searing bolt of jealousy that gave her an inkling of what Stephen might have felt.

'Thanks, but I prefer to make my judgments based on

first-hand information rather than second-hand opinion,' she said, finally succeeding in releasing the door-catch and kicking open the door with a fine disregard for several hundred thousand dollars' worth of high-performance vehicle. She tugged at his arm and after a moment of resistance he let her go, leaning across the seat as she scrambled out to deliver his parting shot.

'In that case why don't you ask him *first-hand* the *real* reason he doesn't want you to meet Michael? It's not because Terri won't let him, but because his twisted mind has persuaded him that Michael isn't his son, but *mine*. And unless somebody makes him believe otherwise he's going to end up freezing that little boy right out of his life!'

CHAPTER NINE

KALERA'S hand smoothed nervously down over the stiff folds of her red silk taffeta dress, her eyes skimming over the glittering throng who had responded to Stephen's gilt-edged invitations, most of whom she'd never seen before and doubted she'd recognise again. They crammed the marble-pillared ballroom and milled around on the dance-floor to the live orchestra, spilling out of the open doors onto the wide terraces where flaming torches lit the sumptuous buffet.

Kalera thought she had been prepared for the strain of this formal engagement party but experience was proving her wrong, not least because of the insidious doubts that had crept into her mind to divide and multiply over the past week, filling her with jittery uncertainty about the future.

But she was proud of the fact that despite Duncan's continuing best efforts to panic her into urgency she had not rushed into making any rash decisions. After last Saturday's confrontation she had not flown straight to Stephen with a string of angry and unsubstantiated accusations, which was obviously what Duncan had hoped she would do. She had not dramatically called off the engagement a mere week before the lavish party that Stephen had devoted so much time and energy to organising. Whatever Stephen had done in the past, Kalera did not believe he deserved to be treated so shabbily.

It might be Duncan's way to fling himself headlong at problems and batter them into submission but it wasn't Kalera's. She preferred to withdraw into herself and carefully look at things from every angle before she decided what action to take, to observe and let her conclusions percolate until she was comfortable and confident with her choice. Sometimes, in her experience, problems even faded away when you refused to take them seriously, and stifling fears eased when you gave them a little breathing room.

Alas, this was not one of those times.

At work she had struggled to regain her old equilibrium in the face of unsettling events. Perhaps in revenge for her stubborn silence on the subject of Stephen, Duncan had abruptly made a choice of secretary—a woman who hadn't even been on Kalera's short-list—and with customary speed had installed her the very same day at a desk face to face with Kalera's.

Bettina Fisher was a busty twenty-year-old university drop-out who wore skin-tight clothing and minimal underwear and seemed to have a problem with the concept of alphabetic order. She was thirty minutes late back from lunch on the first day, cheerfully confiding to Kalera that she had been celebrating her new job in the pub, and she had lost at least half a dozen files every day she had worked. Her typing speed was staccato-fast, but so was her mouth. Kalera had gritted her teeth and been as helpful as she was able to be without screaming. Bettina merely proved her point about hasty decisions. Her appointment had been a spur-of-the-moment reaction that Duncan would live to sorely regret.

Kalera confidently predicted that the jolly Bettina would not last a week after her mentor left, despite the shrink-wrapped breasts and bottom that Duncan pretended to admire when he knew Kalera was looking.

The other jarring note at Labyrinth was the beefing up of security, and the introduction of a new level of secrecy that excluded everyone but Bryan Eastman and Duncan from certain parts of the system. As usual, this was taken as a direct challenge by every hacker in the office worthy of the name and bets were laid on the bulletin board as to who would be first to burrow into the inner sanctum. Meanwhile Bryan and Duncan were often to be seen in low-voiced huddles, and, while Kalera was suddenly surplus to requirements after five o'clock, rumours abounded about all-night sessions in the research department.

'More champagne, madam?'

Kalera started, nearly spilling the remainder of her glass. 'Oh, yes, please,' she said, holding it out to the white-gloved waiter as he topped her up. 'Thank you.' She flushed slightly, belatedly remembering that Stephen had said it wasn't necessary to thank the hired help constantly—one just ignored them and took their excellent service for granted.

She turned back to the room, sipping the perfectly chilled vintage, enjoying the brief period of respite offered by the conveniently large floral arrangement furnished with drooping red spikes of flowers almost the same shade of crimson as her dress. She knew she should be out there circulating, presenting herself for inspection by Stephen's friends, and the movers and shakers of his world who were seizing this chance to mix business with pleasure, but she had been doing it now for nearly two hours and her throat ached from the strain of talking over the top of the conversational rumble.

The men almost without exception were all in black ties but the women were dressed in a myriad of colours and styles, all excruciatingly high fashion, and yet as a group there was a sameness about them that was rather depressing. She caught a flutter of feather and lace amongst the glitter of sequins and silk and smiled reluctantly. Maybe not quite *all* the same. Silver and Kris were here, making their presence felt by their extremely liberal interpretation of 'dress: formal', and frankly making the most of the free food and drink and the chance to spread a little revolutionary talk amongst the scions

of the local establishment. Poor Madeline had nearly
fainted at the sight of Kris's ceremonial blue caftan but
she had been too shrewd to let their guests see her dismay and had minimised the social damage by gushingly
emphasising their status as amusing eccentrics. Once
Kalera might have cringed but tonight she felt only
amusement, unable to shake the strange detachment that
made her feel as if she was a spectator at a play.

Kalera took another, longer gulp of champagne as she
saw Stephen step in from one of the terraces, his blond
head beginning a sweeping search that would inevitably
result in her discovery. He would be annoyed that she
had chosen to lurk in the background instead of basking
in the spotlight but she would weather his disapproval.
He had to accept her for what she was...or not at all.

She studied his tall, handsome figure, radiating boyish
charm as he smoothly worked the room, blatantly enjoying being the focus of attention. Yes, there was something still very boyish about Stephen, an element of nar-
cissistic self-absorption which she had overlooked in her
eagerness to enjoy the security of his affections, and re-
live the joy of being needed. But in spite of Duncan's
dire pronouncements and predictions she still couldn't
bring herself to feel threatened by Stephen's over-
attentive behaviour. Irritated and uncomfortable, perhaps, but not threatened. And that was because there was
not the intensity of emotion between them to generate
such a threat, she had realised in the last few days of
soul-searching, and there probably never would be.
Without passion and ardour to wreak havoc on his self-
control and drive him to try and reimpose control in
other ways, Stephen was merely going through the mo-
tions of habitualised behaviour. Just as Kalera had seen
him as a safe haven for her reawakening feelings, so she
was for him a haven from his own emotional extremity.

And Kalera had seen for herself, that very morning,

the difference between the Stephen of her experience and the one that Duncan had described.

The standing arrangement had been for her to drive to Stephen's in the early evening for a light meal—to compensate for the late dinner they would be having—and for Kalera to shower and have her hair and face done by Madeline's beautician before she changed into her dress. But Kalera had decided on impulse to drop her clothes over in the afternoon, along with the engagement present she had agonised over choosing, in case they didn't get any privacy later in which to exchange their personal gifts. As it happened she'd discovered that Stephen planned to give her hers when he made the formal announcement after dinner.

She had been about to swing into Stephen's curving drive when she had caught sight of the trio emerging from the front door and had panicked, swerving over to the far side of the street and parking under the shade of a spreading pin oak, slumping down in her seat in case she was spotted.

She'd watched the small boy, stylishly dressed in a green polo shirt and baggy safari shorts, tip back his head to look up at the tall man beside him and say something. The boy's hair was as dark as the man's was blond, but even at this distance, or perhaps *because* she wasn't distracted by detail, Kalera could see an echo of genes in the shape of their heads and the proportions of their bodies, and stiff set of their shoulders that denoted both yearning and rejection. If Kalera had harboured any fleeting doubt about Michael's paternity it had been banished then. He could well have been the little boy in those early home videos of Madeline's.

Stephen's hand had raised and Kalera had found herself holding her breath, but instead of a pat on the shoulder or a ruffling of hair there had been a solemn shaking of hands. The boy's thin shoulders were visibly drooping as he'd headed slowly down the stairs towards the silver BMW parked on the gravel.

The slim brunette in the cream sheath, who had been standing behind the two males, had tossed the cigarette she had been jerkily smoking over the balustrade and started to follow, but she'd suddenly whirled around, obviously at some remark, and remounted the stairs to issue a flow of words at Stephen, punctuated by angry, darting gestures with her head and hands.

Whatever she was saying had been like a match to paper for Stephen had ignited into a tempestuous answering volley and for several minutes they had been toe-to-toe in a super-heated exchange. It had ended when Terri threw out her arms and turned away in disgust, only to have Stephen catch her hand and spin her back, jerking her against him for a furious kiss. Reduced to the role of reluctant voyeur, Kalera had felt a rush of embarrassment as she'd watched their angry bodies clash in hostile passion. They had quickly broken away from each other, but she'd been left with a distinct impression of unfinished business.

Kalera had waited until well after the silver BMW had zoomed angrily away before she'd ventured in. Taken aback by her unexpected arrival, Stephen had been distinctly edgy, but he'd soon relaxed when she'd presented him with his engraved gold cuff-links and tie-pin, sufficiently for her to do some gentle probing that finally elicited a casual mention of his ex-wife's visit.

'Did Michael come, too?' she had asked innocently.

'Yes, but they didn't stay long. Terri knows our engagement party is tonight so she chooses today to insist I perform my fatherly duties. She knew I wouldn't have time to spare for the boy. She just wanted to make trouble—'

'And did she succeed?'

Stephen's light brown eyes had been soothing, but his smile was forced. 'Only if she causes us to get into an unpleasant discussion about her, and, believe me, I find every discussion about Terri unpleasant.' That had been an oblique reference to her attempts earlier in the week to encourage him on the subject, when he had simply told her, without the slightest trace of irony, that she had no need to be jealous. 'Forget about Terri. This is supposed to be *our* day...'

Any chance for further serious discussion had been denied as the party designer arrived, twittering about last-minute alterations to the decor requested by Madeline, and the caterers and florist had begun to-ing and fro-ing. Amidst all the bustling activity, Kalera had been discreetly made to feel not only superfluous, but in the way. Stephen had shooed her back home, advising her to spend the afternoon quietly resting so that she would be fresh for the big night ahead.

'Kalera?' Stephen had finally found her and with an obedient smile Kalera moved forward to take his extended hand.

'What are you doing over here? I've been looking for you.'

'Well, I'm here now,' she said, letting him tuck her arm through his and guide her back into the throng.

A passing matron jogged her elbow and she gave a tiny cry as a few sparkles of champagne bounced out of her glass and beaded on the tight bodice of her dress.

'Oh, no, I hope it doesn't mark the silk,' she murmured anxiously, flicking them away with a finger.

'Since you won't be wearing that dress again I wouldn't worry about it,' said Stephen tersely, and Kalera bit the inside of her lip to stop a hasty reply. What could she say?

The dress had been another unfortunate omen for the evening.

She had been stunned when it had been delivered to the house that morning in a tissue-lined black box embossed with the gold symbol of a leading couturier along

with a small slip of paper printed in a flowingly ornate
font.

*I know you've already bought a dress, but when I saw
this one I just knew it was for you. I don't want you
to thank me, this is not my engagement gift, but
please, wear it for me tonight—so that everyone can
appreciate the richness of your beauty as I do...*

The dress she had already bought for the occasion was
a long, shimmering, beaded blue creation, which Kalera
had thought would fit the understated elegance that
Stephen liked to project.

But when she'd opened the box and lifted out the red
taffeta dress she'd found that he had a very different
image of her in mind. She had never worn red before
but the knee-length dress with its draped skirt and rav-
ishingly low sweetheart neckline and small, stand-up ruff
at the back of her neck proved a dramatic foil for her
pale blondeness. And—the most thoughtful and romantic
touch of all—he had sent her matching *shoes*, exactly
the right size for her small feet. Her hesitancy about
accepting such an extravagant gift when her feelings
about her engagement were becoming increasingly am-
bivalent had dissolved when she had tried it on for the
mirror. The silk felt sleekly sensuous against her skin
and the dress itself was pure fashion—dashingly sexy
yet with loads of class. Wearing it had made her feel
almost defiantly confident and she had put the blue creation back in her wardrobe with scarcely a qualm.

But when she had proudly descended the stairs to
meet a few of Stephen's close friends for drinks before
the party proper began the look on Stephen's face as
he'd crossed the foyer to meet her had not been one of
delighted admiration.

'I thought you said you were wearing a long dress?'

he'd said through his teeth as she'd reached the bottom of the curving marble staircase.

'You must have known I wouldn't be able to resist this.' She had smiled back, disconcerted by the white rim around his compressed lips. 'Especially after I read your note.'

'What note?' His hard gaze had shifted to the curving expanse of creamy flesh revealed by the dramatic plunge of red silk between her tightly encased breasts. 'I've never seen you wear that colour,' he'd accused, shortening their steps to keep them out of earshot of the early guests gathered around the sideboard of drinks in the library. 'Or a neckline so low it's almost indecent. What on earth got into you to think it was suitable?'

It had hit her then—the drama of the dress, the whimsy of the impulsive gesture that was so totally unlike him! 'Oh, God,' she said, her hand on his arm bringing him to a full halt. 'You didn't send me this dress?'

Underneath the blandly handsome façade he was furious. 'No, I didn't send it to you! Are you telling me you let someone else buy you a dress?'

'It arrived this morning. The note asking me to wear it wasn't signed. I—well, naturally I thought it was from you,' she protested, aware of his friends' amused glances from the library. No doubt they thought the murmured conversation in the hall was a romantic exchange of sweet nothings.

'A dress that gaudy and you thought it was from *me*?' Stephen heaved a stentorian breath through his nose.

Gaudy! Her newly defiant confidence helped her field that punishing pitch. It was not so much his taste that was offended, but his pride.

'It's not gaudy, it's a very expensive designer dress.' She didn't dare mention the shoes!

Nor did she care to mention the only person who would dare send her a horrendously expensive designer outfit with an anonymous note that implied it was from her fiancé.

But Stephen didn't need telling.

'It has to be bloody Duncan!' he said in a savage undertone. 'I'm not having you wearing anything that bastard bought for you! You'll have to go back up and change!'

'I can't; I haven't got another dress here.' She nudged him into remembering his restive guests. 'Besides, your friends have already seen me in this one. What does it matter, anyhow? No one is going to know—'

'*I'll* know,' Stephen ground out.

Kalera couldn't blame him for being resentful when he had his nose rubbed in his unwelcome knowledge many times during the early course of the evening as she was inundated with compliments about her stunning gown and womanly curiosity about where she had bought it.

Her fingers stilled now on the fading champagne splashes as her ring caught the light of the overhead chandeliers and flashed like an icy beacon against the fiery silk. Fire and ice, she thought. Two radically different elements which could cancel each other out. Fire could melt ice and ice could smother fire...

She shivered.

'Stephen, are you sure we're doing the right thing?' The soft sigh slipped involuntarily out of her mouth and she hastily checked to make sure the betraying words hadn't been overheard.

She saw a fleeting panic blur his brown eyes. 'For God's sake, Kalera—is this just because of that damned dress?' he said roughly. 'I can buy you a hundred other designer dresses to replace it!' He looked at his watch as the orchestra struck up another tune. 'We'll make the formal announcement after this next set,' he said, shifting a small, flat case from his breast to his hip pocket. Her gift, she guessed, and unmistakably jewellery—the same as hers to him. Could neither of them think of anything more interesting?

The conversation around them abruptly dropped, wallowing in a peculiar flat patch that made Kalera look curiously around.

Duncan Royal stood on the threshold of the ballroom, resplendent in black dress trousers and a white dress shirt with concealed buttons—no jacket, and his gold tapestry waistcoat flared open to reveal a red and gold cummerbund...

But it wasn't Duncan who had caused the dramatic hush, it was the woman at his side—even more resplendent in a gold lamé gown which clung to every hint and nuance of her statuesque body.

Terri.

Kalera felt a surge of fury, followed by a terrible desire to laugh.

Stephen was poleaxed, but for only a brief instant. Then his hand clipped around Kalera's free wrist and he dragged her across the room, her glass spilling champagne at every stumbling step, oblivious to a ripple of nervous titters.

'How the hell did you get in?' he snarled, as soon as he got within striking distance of the couple in the doorway.

Duncan hadn't taken his all-encompassing gaze off Kalera as they approached. His eyes were hot with triumph, smouldering with approval as they flirted with the sweetheart neckline and caressed her round breasts and narrow waist, the silken flare of her hips and the peep of her knees beneath the red hem. It was the kind of greedy, needy look that struck delicious terror into her heart.

He took his time in completing his slow appraisal before turning his head to answer Stephen.

'With this.' He produced a gilt invitation seemingly from nowhere with the flick of his wrist, like a magician doing a card trick, and Stephen let go of Kalera to snatch it out of his hand, condemning it with a frown.

'Clever, but still a forgery!' He tore it across and contemptuously tossed the pieces aside.

Duncan shrugged. 'Prove it.' His smile became a taunt. 'Come on, Stephen. As the saying goes, we have the technology. We can prove just about anything in a laboratory these days...providing, of course, that we *want* to prove something that might explode our own speculative theories.'

Only the four of them recognised the challenge for what it was: a veiled reference to the question of Michael's paternity. Kalera clutched her champagne to her chest. Duncan had told her that out of angry pride Terri had refused to agree to a DNA test. Had she now given up hope that Stephen would ever accept his son—or her word—on trust?

Stephen ignored him, turning on his ex-wife, reminding Kalera of their confrontation on the front steps. 'How dare you think you can come and go here as you please?' He vibrated with anger. 'You no longer live here, remember? And how dare you bring *him* here and subject us to a scene?'

'You're the one making a scene out of it, honey,' Terri interrupted in a smoky voice. 'Hi,' she greeted Kalera pleasantly. 'I'm Terri, as you might have gathered, and you're Kalera.' She held out a beautifully kept hand and Kalera dumbly shook it. 'Have we missed Stephen's big speech? Do I offer my congratulations yet?'

'We're about to make the announcement shortly,' Stephen said tightly. 'But you're certainly not going to stay for it. This is utterly and completely tasteless behaviour, even for *you*.'

Terri shrugged, her lamé gown rippling like a waterfall. 'What do I have to lose?' She ran her fingers through her bobbed hair and began a sinuous sway to the music. 'Are you going to offer me a dance?'

Kalera was horribly fascinated by the unfolding scene. Never in a million years would she have expected Stephen to react so intemperately in public.

'No, I am not!' he bit out.

'Not even for old times' sake?'

'If you're doing it for old times' sake, shouldn't you be asking Royal to dance?' he sneered.

Duncan bestirred himself from his lazy-eyed perusal of Kalera. 'I thought I'd keep your fiancée from feeling lonely while you two took your waltz down memory lane.'

Stephen's muscles bunched under the sleek dinner jacket. 'Shut up, you bastard—unless you're asking for a punch in the mouth!'

Terri laid a gold-tipped finger on his arm. 'For goodness' sake, Stephen, all I'm suggesting is that you act like a civilised human being. You've already drawn everyone's attention; what do you want them to see—a boringly amiable encounter between exes, or a knock-down, drag-out fight that will have people gossiping for weeks?'

As a choice it was no choice at all and soon Kalera found herself standing alone with Duncan watching her tense-jawed fiancé and his scheming ex-wife dancing off into the crowd.

'She does know how to manage him,' Duncan remarked admiringly. 'Now if only he could learn to manage *himself* half as well...' He paused before adding, 'Attractive couple, aren't they?'

The fact that they were rubbed salt in the wound.

'*Ex*-couple,' corrected Kalera tartly, giving him a fulminating look, and he reached over and guided her glass to his mouth, his hand covering hers as he took a sip, watching her over the narrow rim.

Other people were probably watching them, too, and Kalera fought to keep her dainty features serenely unembarrassed. She tried to ease away, but he merely followed, still sipping, until she inadvertently backed into a pillar and knew herself squarely trapped.

'Delicious,' he said, smacking his lips as he released the glass, and she knew he wasn't talking about the champagne. He wore a large ruby stud in the Nehru collar of his shirt and a thick hoop of gold in his ear, and with his long midnight hair and swarthy skin he looked as if he would have been every bit as comfortable plying a nefarious trade in the Spanish Main as he was today at conjuring computers to do his bidding.

'I'm glad you wore my sexy little dress,' he told her softly, propping one hand on the pillar above her golden head. 'I was afraid you might resist the temptation and swaddle yourself from head to toe in something pretty, but sadly unadventurous.'

A perfect description of her blue dress!

'I wore this for Stephen,' she said quickly. 'Not for you.'

'You wore it for the man who gave it to you, whoever you might have *thought* it was—and that's me,' he said with satisfaction, hooking a glass of champagne for himself from a passing waiter. 'I spent ages hunting for exactly the right one…one that would warm your skin and furl your body like a half-opened rose…perfumed, velvety-soft, sensual, and alluring…'

God, he was so good with words! Kalera took a deep, steadying breath and his navy eyes dropped to her breasts, the upper curves so pale that the blue veins were visible through her translucent skin. 'I think I can see your heart beating,' he murmured in quick fascination. 'See that little throb there, just below that tiny freckle…'

Kalera was amazed her heart wasn't leaping out of her chest. 'Will you stop leering at me like that?' she choked, blushing like the rose he had described. 'People will notice.'

'I wasn't leering, I was looking.'

'Well, look somewhere else, then!' she hissed.

He grinned down at her. 'You're rather asking for trouble inviting me to do that, aren't you? There are all sorts of delectable parts of you that I'd love to stare at for hours. Like your cute little—'

'*Duncan!*' She passed off a weak smile to a passing legal bigwig, hoping he hadn't heard that last remark.

He touched her hair, lightly, as if he couldn't help himself, and then her drop-pearl earring, making it swing from her velvety lobe. 'Well, how about a dance, then, if you don't want to talk?' he invited huskily. 'Then I won't be able to look any further than your face. Or we can both just close our eyes and hold each other.'

The idea filled her with panic. The few times he had got his arms around her she had completely lost her head and ended up in a turmoil of guilt and self-contempt.

'Look, I know you're just playing an *agent provocateur*—' she began raggedly.

'Is that really what you think of me?' he interrupted. 'You think I'm the kind of man who would tempt you to illegal acts solely in order to disgrace you?'

He actually sounded hurt. 'Not illegal, but certainly *immoral*,' she said, shaken by the thought of *her* causing *him* pain.

'There's nothing immoral about love—it's one of the truly great splendours of life...'

Kalera's grey eyes clouded as she fought off the seductive notion of Duncan splendidly in love. He was talking about the physical act between lovers, not the deep emotional commitment between two people, she reminded herself, and it was an attitude she would never let herself share. 'There's a personal sense of right and wrong that governs *everything* we do...'

She looked away, trying to escape the hypnotic intensity of his concentration, and her whole body tensed with alarm.

'Oh, God!'

Duncan followed her gaze to where Stephen and Terri

were squaring off again, this time in the middle of the dance-floor.

'Oh, *no*!'

Duncan caught her elbow as she tried to dart past him. 'Where do you think you're going?'

'Look at them! We have to stop them—'

He shook his head, his grip tightening. 'Stay out of the way. This isn't your fight. Don't get involved.'

'Don't get *involved*?' She twisted her arm free and flashed her ring angrily in his face. 'What do you think this is? I'm already *involved*!'

'Not in this you're not. Look at them, Kalera—they're too wrapped up in themselves to give a damn about anything else right now. They don't care what they're doing to you. You know what happens when you try to separate fighting dogs—you're likely to get a mauling yourself!'

Kalera shrugged off his callous advice, thrusting her glass into the hand that was trying to detain her and not looking back. He would love it if Stephen made a complete idiot of himself; that was probably why he had brought Terri along. God knew what they were saying to each other over there, but it was probably nothing Stephen wanted other people to hear. If he was thinking straight he wouldn't dream of washing his dirty linen in public. She owed it to him to stop their argument escalating before the whole room became aware of what was going on. He would never forgive himself if he turned this evening of supposed joy into a domestic tragicomedy.

Kalera threaded her way towards them, trying to pin on a sophisticated smile of wry amusement but aware that it kept slipping into a grimace. Just as she reached the ring of people closest to the combat zone there were gasps as Terri slapped Stephen's face, swung on her heel and fled out onto the terrace and down the steps, a glimmering wraith disappearing into the garden.

'Terri? Come back here! Terri!' Without hesitation Stephen dived after her, almost pushing Kalera over in his haste, completely ignoring her attempt to talk to him, his furious gaze passing straight through her as if she didn't exist.

Standing there, staring after the fleeing couple, Kalera could feel the bubbling black acid of humiliation burning up in her throat. She could hear the groundswell of shocked whispers and feel the scorch of pitying stares. Her slender back stiffened to the point of snapping and, very carefully placing one foot in front of the other, her head held high, she began to walk back the way she had come.

At some point Duncan joined her on the endless journey through the void of her embarrassment and with his arm around her back she found the strength to obey his instruction to talk and smile and even laugh with him as if nothing were wrong.

'Great, you're doing great; we're almost there,' he praised as their shoes clicked across the marble foyer towards the massive oak front door.

'Almost where? What are we doing?' she said, her steps beginning to falter.

'Leaving.'

Some vestige of social conscience in her baulked as the dinner-jacketed security guard opened the door. 'I can't run out on my own engagement party!'

'Why not? Stephen did. And he left you standing there to face the fallout.'

The scalding embarrassment rushed back in full measure and with it a healthy, invigorating anger.

He tossed his car keys lightly in his hand. 'Besides, do you really want to hang around like a good little girl, meekly making nice-nice to all *his* guests and *his* friends while you wait for him to deign to remember that he has a fiancée?'

She reached out and caught the falling keys. 'No, I

don't,' she said crisply. 'Let's go. And this time *I'll* do the driving!'

His face blanched and a surge of cleansing humour bubbled through her veins, diluting the hurt. She tossed the keys under *his* nose before she fisted them and sauntered past him out of the door.

Let *him* find out something of what it was like to find your life recklessly careering away with you at high speed with no sense of control over the outcome!

CHAPTER TEN

ARRIVING at the office on the Monday morning after her disastrous engagement party, Kalera found herself walking into a whirlwind. At first she thought the turmoil meant there must have been a fire alarm.

'What's happening?' she asked Luke, one of the software engineers, as he staggered down the hallway with an armload of portable hard-disk drives and cartridges.

'We're bugging out,' he grinned.

'*Moving?*' she asked incredulously. They couldn't have been evicted because Duncan owned the building! 'What—everyone?'

'Nah. Just the A-team.'

That meant Bryan Eastman's lot.

'Where are you going?'

'Dunno…the roof first, then no one's saying. A distant galaxy far, far away is my guess.'

'The *roof*!' Kalera hurried down to her office, which was in equal chaos, but not because of any moving.

'What's going on, Bettina?'

'I don't know; no one tells me anything,' the young woman complained, rummaging in the files, yelping when she almost broke a nail. 'Hey, have you seen the Bredon disk? I was sure I put it somewhere in here on Friday.'

'Have you checked under B?'

Bettina looked at her blankly and Kalera left before she gave in to the overwhelming desire to fire her on the spot. Her feet slowing, she headed towards Duncan's door. There was no sense in putting off this confrontation any longer.

Duncan was pacing up and down insulting someone over his mobile phone, darting over every now and then to punch an addition into the open laptop on his desk. His light grey suit would have been numbingly plain but for the effect of the lime-green shirt and an electrifying fluorescent green tie sprinkled with little orange lightning bolts. When he looked up and saw Kalera something flared in his eyes and he hastily ended his call and slammed the phone down on the desk.

'You're late!' he barked.

It was not the manner of greeting she had expected, and it immediately put her on familiar ground.

'I had trouble with my car,' she said mildly.

'I thought you weren't going to turn up at all,' he growled, explaining his ill humour, his eyes running over her as if to make sure she was all there. She had her neat, practical office garb on again and looked a world away from the woman she had been on Saturday night. *His* world, he thought, with a gloating surge of satisfaction.

He gave her a brilliant smile. 'Not the twins again?'

She sighed. He probably wouldn't give up until he had dragged it out of her. 'I ran out of petrol.'

His eyes widened. 'On the way to work? You? Mrs Organisation herself?'

'I used the car a lot over the weekend,' she said unsmilingly, 'and I had other things on my mind.'

His frown was swift to reappear. 'Yes, where were you yesterday? I tried you at home, and at your parents'. I wanted to make sure you were all right.'

Shades of Stephen! 'I was fine,' she said, with a little tilt of her chin that told him it was a lie. 'I went for a drive.'

'All day and night?' His scowl deepened. 'I even rang Steve's place but I never got anything but the answering machine. I thought you and he might have been meeting somewhere…?'

'Well, we weren't. I drove lots of places, and I stopped at a motel for the night.' As an anonymous traveller—out of reach of people or telephones, and free of sympathy, advice or any kind of pressure. 'I just wanted some time on my own.'

His dark brows lifted. 'So...' He moved towards her, tense with expectancy. 'Have you and Steve settled things between you?'

She shook her head and gestured helplessly with her hands, bringing him to a halt as his eyes zeroed in on what Anna had seen.

'We hardly had a chance for more than a few words, when I went to pick up my car.' And those composed of futile counter-recriminations, with Stephen even suggesting that *she* was the one who had overreacted on Saturday night. 'Stephen was rushing out to the hospital because apparently Michael fell down some stairs early yesterday morning, and got a slight concussion and a badly broken arm. Maybe Stephen spent all day at the hospital; I don't know.' Perhaps the trauma had succeeded in jolting him into recognising the unbreakable emotional bond he shared with his son. For both their sakes, Kalera hoped so.

Duncan picked up her right hand, thumbing the ostentatious ring. 'He never did get to make that announcement, did he? So you could say you're not formally engaged at all...'

'We're not formally *dis*engaged either,' she said warily.

His grip tightened. 'But you will be soon?' he insisted.

A familiar look of stubbornness entered her grey eyes as she resisted his coercion. She had no intention of telling him that the ring was on her finger simply because it was the safest place to keep it. She didn't want to make herself any more vulnerable than she was already.

'I can't say,' she prevaricated, firmly extracting her

hand. 'I need to see Stephen first. In fact, I'm going to go over there this evening,' she decided.

'You can't!' he rapped out.

The command made her raise haughty eyebrows. 'I beg your pardon?'

Anna's head poked around the corner. 'Hey, Chief, Bryan says you'd better suit up—it's zero-minus-ten and counting.'

'All right, all right—' He waved her away and began grabbing things off his desk and slinging them into a briefcase.

'What on earth is going on?'

He snapped down the catches on the briefcase and spun the combination lock. 'Get your laptop and come with me.'

'What for?' she asked, relieved to turn her mind to more impersonal matters.

'Just do it, OK?' he said impatiently.

'Where are we going?'

'You'll find out when we get there—like all the rest.'

There was safety in numbers, she reminded herself. 'Are we going to be away long?'

'Probably.'

'You're going to leave Bettina in charge of the office for the whole day?' was her first appalled thought.

'Anna'll keep her in line. Now can you get a move on? Everyone else is waiting…'

He hustled her into the lift and pressed the button for the top floor.

On the windy roof Kalera stared in dismay at the helicopter being loaded up by Bryan and his four co-workers, all of whom, she noticed ominously, had roll-bags or suitcases of personal gear.

'Exactly how long is *long*?' she demanded as Duncan added his briefcase and laptop to the load.

He shrugged. 'However long it takes. Look—' he tersely cut off her burgeoning protest '—your *soon-to-*

be-ex-fiancé—' the emphasis was crushing '—has suddenly started boasting about a speech-recognition program which bears a suspicious resemblance to ours, so I'm cutting off any possible source of information. I'm going to sequester this team in a leak-proof fortress and maybe, without any outside distractions, we can accelerate our final debugging and bring this baby home early enough to pre-empt a coup.'

'Why take me and not Anna?'

'Because Anna's working on other priority programs and I'd rather have *you* where I can keep an eye on you…'

'Are you accusing me of having something to do with the leak?' She bristled up at him.

'If I thought *that* you wouldn't have a ticket to ride,' he said, throttling her doubt with a look.

'Then how come everyone but me got more than five minutes' notice?' she said, pointing at the pile of suitcases.

'Because I was able to contact all of *them* yesterday,' said Duncan smoothly.

'But I haven't made any arrangements to be away.' She chafed. 'I haven't even got a change of clothes! And what about my car—and my house? I have to cancel the paper!'

'Anna is going to deal with all that for you. You can send her a message about what things to pack for you and we'll send the helicopter back to collect it.' The wind had whipped his black hair into devilish quiffs.

'I should at least let my parents know I'll be away—'

'Already done.'

She hesitated, twisting the burdensome ring on her finger, before admitting the root of her reluctance. It was no good—she couldn't leave herself, or Stephen, hanging in limbo for an indeterminate length of time…

'I need to make *one* phone call,' she pleaded, hoping

that Stephen would be in his office. 'It won't take long—'

The pilot had begun to rotate the huge blades.

'No time,' said Duncan flatly. 'Sorry.'

Kalera didn't think he looked very sorry.

'Are you sure it's safe to take off in this wind? It seems pretty gusty.' Her voice lifted to compete with the rising throb of the blades.

'It landed, didn't it? Come on, Kalera, any woman who can drive an F1 the way you did on Saturday night can't be afraid of a little breeze.'

Kalera pushed at the hem of her skirt as the swirling air stirred up by the helicopter flipped it up her thighs. It still unnerved her to remember how power-crazed she had acted when she had got behind the wheel of his ridiculously expensive macho-machine.

The sexy purr of the engine, the roar of the tyres on the road and the wind past her open window, and the sweet vibration of all that power, had been an exhilarating combination. With Duncan gritting his teeth in the passenger seat she had cruised through the suburbs, getting used to the superb handling, and then planted her foot down on the motorway with reckless disregard for the speed-camera signs.

When Duncan had kindly pointed them out she had laughed. It was *his* car...if she was flashed, then the traffic department would be sending *him* the fine—and it would be a small price to pay for all the trouble he had caused!

She had driven eighty kilometres out into the country before she'd turned around, and by the time they'd made the outskirts of the city again most of her anger had been dissipated in the concentration it had required to navigate the dark roads. Easing off the pedal, she had taken an off-ramp at random and Duncan had unclamped his hands from the edge of his seat and croaked, 'Where to now?'

Kalera ducked her head to read a fluorescent street name. 'I'm not sure—I don't know where we are…'

'I do. Why don't you let me—?' She shot him a searing look and he altered his next word before it issued from his mouth. 'Navigate from here.'

'I'm not going to your place,' she warned fiercely. She had made enough mistakes for one night.

'Fine…' His face was calm, as if no such thought had even entered his head. 'Take the next left, and then go right, at the intersection…'

When he finally directed her through huge, twin stone pillars and up a narrow road lined with box hedges she was completely mystified by his choice of destination.

'What is this place—a museum?' she murmured, parking where instructed and looking up at the classical stone building, its exterior softly illuminated by concealed spotlights in the formal shubbery that ran along the frontage. There were also lights showing through the downstairs windows.

'It's the house where I grew up. My parents live here.' He unclipped his seat belt, and then hers, leaning over to flick off the headlights. 'We're probably just in time to join them for coffee and liqueurs—they like to keep fashionably late hours.'

She gaped at him as he got out and walked around the front of the car to open her door.

'You brought me here to see your *parents*?' she squeaked.

He bent down to offer her his hand. 'You took me to see *yours*—'

'You invited yourself!'

'Well, now I'm inviting *you*.'

'I can't go in there *now*!' she said feverishly, shrinking back into her seat.

'Why not? They don't know what's happened,' he said, prising her out. 'And what better time to meet people than when you're dressed to impress? Aren't you the least bit curious about my background?'

In truth she was fascinated, but half an hour later Kalera had satisfied her curiosity and was dying to leave.

Jacob and Serena Royal were both handsome, highly educated, articulate and opinionated. They were also amongst the most boring people that Kalera had ever met. Their lack of humour made the conversation turgid and their subtly domineering attitude towards their son made Kalera inwardly bristle on his behalf.

'If you'd gone to the Bar you probably would have taken Silk by now,' was all his father said when Duncan mentioned a recent Labyrinth product which had won a leading computer magazine award. It was evident from their condescension that Duncan's brilliance and success in a field for which his parents had little respect or understanding meant less to them than the academic failures and peripatetic nature of his past. Kalera felt a surge of gratefulness that he had managed to escape the straitjacket of conformity into which his mother and father had tried to force him.

Perched on the edge of an uncomfortable antique sofa, balancing a wafer-thin cup of Colombian coffee on her knee, Kalera weathered another quarter of an hour of excruciatingly dull conversation before Duncan blandly asked if she could bear to tear herself away.

When the door shut behind them they both uttered identical, deep sighs of relief and their eyes met in an exquisite moment of perfect understanding. Duncan grinned and she realised that he hadn't smiled once inside the stultifying solemnity of that house.

'Freedom!' He caught up her hand and together they ran down to the car, laughing, like two children escaping school for the summer.

Without discussion, Duncan took the wheel, surprising her yet again when they ended up at a regional park high on the cliffs overlooking Waitemata Harbour.

There were a few other cars parked on the access road, a lovers' lane of steamy windows, but Duncan drove past them, over a cattle grid and up to a dead end where a wire fence supported a wooden stile. There he took off his shoes and socks and made Kalera do the same, teasing her as she made him turn his back for her to unroll her stockings, and walked her across the rolling, moonlit fields, the grass already damp with spring dew, to where the sea breeze met the edge of the cliff, throwing up a salt-perfumed gush of air.

'I love coming up here alone late at night,' he exulted softly, tipping his head back to stare up at the vast vault of heaven pricked with stars. 'Just me...and the rest of the universe.'

The light from the yellow slice of moon was just enough to silver his strongest features, throwing the rest into impenetrable shadow.

'You can dream dreams here with no one to tell you that they're futile or feckless. Someone once told me that the way to success is never to stop believing in your dreams, or trying to achieve them...'

Kalera wrapped her arms around herself, soaking up the tranquillity of the night, feeling safe enough under the cover of the darkness to study him for the first time with her heart in her eyes, aching with the knowledge that her own secret dream, the one she had steadfastly refused to admit even to herself, was still as unreachable as the stars overhead. She loved Duncan Royal, had loved him for much longer than was comfortable to contemplate.

'After visiting the family mausoleum,' he murmured, still scanning the heavens, 'you must know why it's always been so important for me to be free—to be a renegade who makes his own rules.'

'Is that why you took me there?' She turned to look out over the shadowy sea, the lights of the distant shore suddenly blurring in her sight.

Oh, God, had he guessed how she felt? Did he think she had required an object lesson on how little to expect from him? She knew him too well to have believed it would be any different. In spite of his flamboyant gregariousness and greedy appetite for excitement, he travelled through life essentially alone. Just Duncan and the universe of dreams he carried inside him.

She felt him move up behind her, his hands steadying the sway of her slight body in the breeze. 'I wanted you to understand. You think we're worlds apart in our outlook but we're not so very different, you and I, in what drives us to do the things that we do and make the choices that we have. Neither of us wants to be our parents...'

'I don't think there's any danger you'll end up like your father,' said Kalera, thinking of the dour, repressive man whose face might have been carved in granite.

His arms replaced his hands, folding around her waist, his chin propped on her moon-silvered top-knot as he drew her securely back against him.

'And you have too much strength of will to ever be swayed into forsaking your responsibilities for the sake of casual self-indulgence, as your mother did.

'You had too much freedom in your childhood, I had too little. We both over-compensated. The trick is to hold a balance in your life.'

'I'd like to learn that trick some day,' sighed Kalera.

He turned her in his arms, a column of moonstruck fire, and rested his cool forehead against hers. 'Would you like me to teach you?' he whispered, nudging her nose with his.

He had obliquely warned her off falling in love with him, and now he was inviting her to accept him for the man he was...

A breath away from being kissed, she lost courage and turned her cheek.

He was not dispirited. 'Ever since your mother told

me you were born on grass I've had this lovely fantasy,' he murmured, nuzzling the silky slant of her delicate cheekbone. 'You naked as the day you were born on a lush field of grass. Will you make love with me, now, Kalera—here on this bed of grass, in the moonlight...?'

If only she had. If only she hadn't been too shocked, too shy, too fearful of betraying her most private emotions to act out his fantasy, maybe she wouldn't be feeling so miserable and confused now...

'Kalera? Are you going to get into that helicopter or are we going to have to winch you in?'

Wrenched back to the present by Duncan's impatient growl, Kalera stumbled forward, bending low, and hitched her skirt to climb into the rear of the transport, gasping as she received a caressing boost to her taut rear by Duncan's cupped hand.

She flushed as she subsided into her seat and was immediately squashed up against the bulkhead by Duncan, who ensured she was buckled in before he issued a thumbs-up to the pilot. The rotation increased sharply and the helicopter shuddered and lurched. Kalera closed her eyes and a warm hand wrapped around her white-knuckled fingers as they swooped off the top of the building. It was several minutes before she opened her eyes and Duncan gave her hand a warm squeeze of reassurance as she looked out of the window, her stomach lurching to see that they were skimming over the sparkling waters of Waitemata Harbour. Soon, though, she was fascinated by the view, eagerly looking out for the landmarks Duncan pointed out in the toy-land unfolding below while Bryan dozed and his four young 'apostles', Matthew, Mark, Luke and Brendan, played a series of wildly fast games of cards that competed against the rotors for rowdiness.

It took an hour to get to their secret destination, flying south across the Firth of Thames to an isolated spot in the south-eastern reaches of the Coromandel Ranges. As

the helicopter hovered low over a cleared patch of land
in the midst of thick native bush, Kalera saw a large,
square, single-storey house of white-washed concrete.

She turned wide grey eyes to Duncan's face.

He nodded, leaning close to her ear to be heard. 'I
call it The Labyrinth.'

'You own it?'

His navy eyes gleamed. 'Built it four years ago. My
secret hideaway from the world...'

Privately she thought it a rather ridiculous name for
such a prosaic dwelling—until she walked through the
ceiling-high front door and discovered that the interior
was constructed as a clever series of square rooms of
various sizes connected by a maze-like interconnection
of corridors which doubled as bookshelves and storage
areas. All the interior doors were internal sliders which
vanished back into the walls, thus preserving the illusion
of endless entrances and exits and providing the option
of open-plan living or very private bolt-holes.

As Duncan trailed his troop of guests across the polished wood floors, introducing them to the intricate lay-
out of the colourfully furnished white-walled rooms,
Kalera murmured, 'It looks sort of like—'

'A labyrinth, I know; I designed it that way.' He rewarded her with an indulgent smile. 'Let me show you
the bedrooms I've allocated for you all and then we can
get settled in. I have a live-in caretaker who is a fantastic
cook, by the way, so anything you want in the kitchen,
just ask Jed—except for snacks and drinks; you can help
yourself to those.'

He showed the five men their sleeping quarters first—
a cluster of twin-bedded rooms next to a fully equipped
computer centre soon cluttered with all the extra equip-
ment they had bought.

Kalera, to her dismay, was far away on the opposite
side of the house, in a spacious bedroom next to
Duncan's.

She looked slowly around her room, her eyes avoiding the sliding door midway along the wall, which she guessed must open into Duncan's master suite, and the wide, inviting bed with its sensuous green satin cover.

'Shouldn't I be over with the rest of the workers?' she commented.

'I wanted you near me,' he said simply, sending a frisson up her spine with his heavy-lidded smile. 'In case I need you.'

She looked at him sharply. 'For work, you mean?'

The smile grew bitter-sweet. 'I can always rely on you to tell me what I mean, can't I, Kalera? God forbid you should believe I mean what I actually say.'

Shortly afterwards the helicopter was despatched on a round trip back to Auckland in order to fetch Kalera's solitary suitcase—an absurd extravagance that she nonetheless accepted as compensation for the vast inconvenience of the trip.

Over the next three days, Kalera saw virtually nothing of the other five men, who seemed to be breathing, eating and sleeping on the job, but she saw far too much of Duncan, whose sole purpose in existing now seemed to be to drive her crazy with unrequited love. Now that she had finally admitted her own feelings to herself, it was proving impossible to push them aside and pretend that she wasn't aware of him with every breath that she took.

It didn't help that instead of knuckling down to any serious work Duncan was merely flirting with it—and with her—teasing her with his arrant mischief, making her laugh at his wit and tempting her with sultry glances and wicked reminders of the passion they had shared.

The catalyst came early one morning when she happened to meet Bryan in a state of half-zombification in the kitchen, blearily chugging milk from the refrigerator after another all-nighter, and learned something from him that sent her exploding furiously into Duncan's bedroom, forgetting she was only wearing her demure white cotton nightie.

He groaned and rolled over onto his back, looking up at the blonde banshee who had erupted into his dreams.

'This is all an elaborate sham, isn't it?' she shouted at his big, supine body, sheathed in green satin sheets. 'We never *had* to come down here at all! Bryan just told me that there *wasn't* a big leak at all, just a campaign of misinformation by Stephen—and you knew all about it last Friday!' Throwing his behaviour at the party into a shattering new perspective and raising all her old angry doubts about his motives.

Duncan closed his eyes again and she was furious with him for pretending to be bored to sleep by her accusations.

'Get up! I want to hear this from *you*. There's no need for us to be here at all, is there?'

She grabbed a handful of the slippery sheet, creased across his chest, and tugged it threateningly. 'I *said*, get *up*, you rat!'

'I wouldn't do that if I were you,' he warned gently, still not opening his eyes.

Exhilaration raced through her veins at the challenge.

'Huh!' With a snort of defiance she ripped the bed-clothes off and tossed them away over the end of the bed where he wouldn't be able to reach them. Her whole body immediately felt as if it had been dipped in boiling water.

'As you can see, I'm already up,' drawled Duncan, looking down at the bold arousal of his body. He lazily rolled onto his side, facing her with the jutting evidence. 'Actually, I'm always up when you're around, Kalera. This happened last time you came into my bedroom, too, remember?'

All too well. She trembled, unable to look away, the turbulent excitement building to flashpoint inside her, the breath jamming in her throat as he lightly touched himself. 'Don't—'

'Don't what? Want you? Too late. Look at me. This is how I feel about you. I want you…all the time. And I've waited a long time for you to invite yourself back into my bedroom…'

She gasped and turned to flee, but he hit the floor running and scooped her up easily with one long, muscled arm, ramming the door shut with a bang, and flipping her backwards onto the crumpled sheet in a wild flurry of long blonde hair and kicking bare legs.

'You want the charade to be over—so be it, it's over!' he said, pinning her to the bed with his sleep-warm body, luxuriating in the instant melting of her resistance. 'Bryan wanted to give the project a hurry-up and this was the perfect place to do a full immersion, but no, you and I didn't have to come, too. You and I are here because of *this*…'

He lifted her right hand and dragged off the glittering diamond ring and threw it onto the floor. Then he placed her bare hand on his thrusting body and crushed her mouth with his and suddenly her dammed emotions were bursting their swollen banks and she was fighting with him for the pleasure, helping him tear off her nightie, arching her breasts to his mouth and lifting her legs to encompass the rock-hard strength of his thighs, guiding him into the silky heat for the physical union that would complete them as two halves of a whole. The intense pleasure spiked at his first thrust, then again, and again, as his hips drove him deep into her central core, and Kalera shuddered, her gasping cry mingling with his answering groan of completion.

'I never meant that to happen,' said Duncan in a hoarse, stunned voice as they lay in a tangle of sweaty glory. He felt her tense beneath him and chuckled wryly into her tangled hair. 'I don't mean making love to you, darling, I mean ravishing you wildly like that. Not the first time. I was going to seduce you gently, with love, so that you'd respect me in the morning—and yourself— not like that other time...'

With love. Her heart suddenly felt too big for her breast. 'I wasn't ready for you then,' she remembered painfully. 'You were too...'

He lifted his head and frowned down into her eyes. 'Too what?'

'Much,' she said wryly, touched by his anxiety. 'Too exciting, too sexy, too...*alive.* Too much a man for me in every way at that point in my life.'

'So you turned to Stephen instead.'

She blushed. 'He was...comfortable. I thought that was what I wanted.'

'And what do you want now?'

With love. She made the final leap of trust. 'You.'

Joy made his eyes very blue. *'I* was ready for you,' he told her quietly. 'I've been ready now for a long, long time, Kalera. Much longer than you imagine. I knew you felt you had betrayed Harry by asking me to make love to you, but *I* didn't feel guilty. I loved it. And, hell, I figured Harry owed me that much...'

'Owed you for what? I thought Harry was your friend.'

'Harry was my friend because he felt sorry for me.'

She was stunned. *'Sorry* for you?'

He smoothed her hair gently back from her forehead. 'He knew that you loved him and he felt sorry for me because he knew how I felt about you. Don't ask me how, since *you* never had a clue, but *he* did. But he didn't come the heavy husband or warn me off—oh, no, not Harry. After that party of yours when you and I danced on the balcony he rang to offer me a round of golf, even though he knew I didn't play. He knew I'd accept, you see—he knew I'd be curious about Kalera's husband.

'I wanted him to be an insensitive bastard who didn't

deserve you, but he wasn't, he was a bloody nice guy. He was utterly secure in who he was. It didn't matter to him that I was better educated, richer, brighter and better-looking than he was—he knew he had the one supreme advantage that I could never top: you loved him. So he made a friend of me when most men would have shunned me as a potential enemy.

'And do you know what else he did?' His voice softened with awe. 'He *trusted* me. He trusted me not to do what he knew I wanted with my whole heart and soul to do...seduce his wife and take her away from him for ever. I wanted you to love *me*, not him, to wear *my* ring with the pride that you wore his, to have *my* babies...'

'Oh, Duncan—' Her throat thickened with love.

'I loved him for that, Kalera,' he said proudly. 'For giving me back the honour that Stephen stole from me. And I loved him because *you* found him worthy of love...because what you love I love.'

'You obviously love yourself very much, then,' she teased tenderly, knowing now that there was emotional security to be found even in loving a turbulent man of extremes. 'But then I always knew you were a dreadful egotist!'

'I was beginning to think I'd never hear you admit you loved me,' he gloated, running his hands over her slender body, and arousing her all over again. 'I hope I'm not going to wake up to find this is just another dream...'

'But it is,' she told him. 'You're my for ever dream, and I'll never stop believing in you...and in us...'

Passion

**Looking for stories that *sizzle*?
Wanting a read that has a little
extra *spice*?**

**Harlequin Presents® is thrilled
to bring you romances that
turn up the heat!**

In March 1999 look out for:

The Marriage Surrender
by Michelle Reid
Harlequin Presents #2014

Every other month throughout 1999,
there'll be a **PRESENTS PASSION** book by one
of your favorite authors: Miranda Lee,
Helen Bianchin, Sara Craven and Michelle Reid!

*Pick up a **PRESENTS PASSION**—
where **seduction** is guaranteed!*

Available wherever Harlequin books are sold.

HARLEQUIN®
Makes any time special ™

Look us up on-line at: http://www.romance.net

HPPAS1-R

If you enjoyed what you just read,
then we've got an offer you can't resist!

Take 2 bestselling love stories FREE!

Plus get a FREE surprise gift!

Clip this page and mail it to Harlequin Reader Service®

IN U.S.A.	IN CANADA
3010 Walden Ave.	P.O. Box 609
P.O. Box 1867	Fort Erie, Ontario
Buffalo, N.Y. 14240-1867	L2A 5X3

YES! Please send me 2 free Harlequin Presents® novels and my free surprise gift. Then send me 6 brand-new novels every month, which I will receive months before they're available in stores. In the U.S.A., bill me at the bargain price of $3.12 plus 25¢ delivery per book and applicable sales tax, if any*. In Canada, bill me at the bargain price of $3.49 plus 25¢ delivery per book and applicable taxes**. That's the complete price and a savings of over 10% off the cover prices—what a great deal! I understand that accepting the 2 free books and gift places me under no obligation ever to buy any books. I can always return a shipment and cancel at any time. Even if I never buy another book from Harlequin, the 2 free books and gift are mine to keep forever. So why not take us up on our invitation. You'll be glad you did!

106 HEN CNER
306 HEN CNES

Name	(PLEASE PRINT)	
Address	Apt.#	
City	State/Prov.	Zip/Postal Code

* Terms and prices subject to change without notice. Sales tax applicable in N.Y.
** Canadian residents will be charged applicable provincial taxes and GST.
  All orders subject to approval. Offer limited to one per household.
  ® are registered trademarks of Harlequin Enterprises Limited.

PRES99   ©1998 Harlequin Enterprises Limited

HARLEQUIN PRESENTS®

This February 1999 celebrate

Valentine's Day

with Harlequin Presents® and

The Sexiest Man Alive

by
Sandra Marton

The Sexiest Man Alive
(Harlequin Presents #2008) is Matt Romano.
He'll be your best Valentine's Day date *ever!*

Available wherever Harlequin books are sold.

HARLEQUIN®
Makes any time special ™

Look us up on-line at: http://www.romance.net   HPVAL

Tough, rugged and irresistible...

THE AUSTRALIANS

Stories of romance Australian-style, guaranteed to fulfill that sense of adventure!

This March 1999 look for
Boots in the Bedroom!
by **Alison Kelly**

Parish Dunford lived in his cowboy boots—no one was going to change his independent, masculine ways. Gina, Parish's newest employee, had no intention of trying to do so—she preferred a soft bed to a sleeping bag on the prairie. Yet somehow she couldn't stop thinking of how those boots would look in her bedroom—with Parish still in them....

The Wonder from Down Under: where spirited women win the hearts of Australia's most independent men!

Available March 1999
at your favorite retail outlet.

HARLEQUIN®
Makes any time special ™

Look us up on-line at: http://www.romance.net

PHAUS9

Coming Next Month

HARLEQUIN PRESENTS®

THE BEST HAS JUST GOTTEN BETTER!

#2013 CONTRACT BABY Lynne Graham
(The Husband Hunters)
Becoming a surrogate mother was Polly's only option when her mother needed a life-saving operation. But the baby's father was businessman Raul Zaforteza, and he would do anything to keep his unborn child—even marry Polly....

#2014 THE MARRIAGE SURRENDER Michelle Reid
(Presents Passion)
When Joanna had no choice but to turn to her estranged husband, Sandro, for help, he agreed, but on one condition: that she return to his bed—as his wife. But what would happen when he discovered her secret?

#2015 THE BRIDE WORE SCARLET Diana Hamilton
When Daniel Faber met his stepbrother's mistress, Annie Kincaid, he decided the only way he could keep her away from his stepbrother was to kidnap her! But the plan had a fatal flaw—Daniel had realized he wanted Annie for himself!

#2016 DANTE'S TWINS Catherine Spencer
(Expecting!)
It wasn't just jealous colleagues who believed Leila was marrying for money; so did her boss, and fiancé Dante Rossi! How could Leila marry him without convincing him she was more than just the mother of his twins?

#2017 ONE WEDDING REQUIRED! Sharon Kendrick
(Wanted: One Wedding Dress)
Amber was delighted to be preparing to marry her boss, hunky Finn Fitzgerald. But after she gave an ill-advised interview to an unscrupulous journalist, it seemed there wasn't going to be a wedding at all....

#2018 MISSION TO SEDUCE Sally Wentworth
Allie was certain she didn't need bodyguard Drake Marsden for her assignment in Russia. But Drake refused to leave her day or night, and then he decided that the safest place for her was in his bed!

HARLEQUIN CELEBRATES

FIVE DECADES OF ROMANCE

With Harlequin there's a romance to fit your every mood.

Choose the one that's right for you!

PASSION
Harlequin Presents
Harlequin Temptation

TENDER LOVE STORIES
Harlequin Romance

HOME & FAMILY
Harlequin
American Romance

HUMOR
Harlequin Love & Laughter

A LONGER STORY WITH MORE
Harlequin Superromance

SUSPENSE/ ADVENTURE
Harlequin Intrigue

HISTORICAL
Harlequin Historicals

Look us up on-line at: http://www.romance.net   H50L